REVOLUTION BABY

Joanna Gruda

REVOLUTION BABY

*Translated from the French
by Alison Anderson*

Europa
editions

Europa Editions
214 West 29th Street
New York, N.Y. 10001
www.europaeditions.com
info@europaeditions.com

Library of Congress Cataloging in Publication Data is available
ISBN 978-1-60945-198-1

We acknowledge the financial support of the Government of Québec through
La Société de développement des entreprises culturelles (SODEC).

Gruda, Joanna
Revolution Baby

Book design by Emanuele Ragnisco
www.mekkanografici.com
Cover photo © Keystone-France/Getty

Prepress by Grafica Punto Print – Rome
Printed in the USA

To Julek, thanks a thousand times over for your thrilling life
To Geneviève, who loved children with periwinkle eyes

REVOLUTION BABY

PROLOGUE

When I was little, I had parents. And an aunt and an uncle, too. Later, I was put in an orphanage. And there was the war, the same as for everyone. After the war, I had parents. And an aunt and an uncle, too. But not the same ones as before.

My story begins on March 17, 1929. It was a very important day for me, because that was the day my existence was put to the vote.

There we were in Moscow, in the middle of a meeting of a Polish Communist Party cell. Third matter on the agenda: Comrade Helena Rappoport's pregnancy. Might she be allowed to continue in her state of gravidity, or must she undergo an abortion? The debate was lively. Some people took a very dim view of her pregnancy, for it might incite other women caught up in the struggle for the proletarian revolution to reproduce (an act considered to be highly anti-revolutionary during those troubled years). Then there were those who believed that it was a good idea to bring future revolutionaries into the world, offspring who would know how to carry on the work they had all committed to. The response to the latter was that they were taking a pessimistic view of the future, for it was obvious that when these children were old enough to take part in the class struggle, communism would already have conquered the majority of European countries. Comrade Helena Rappoport and the other comrades with procreative designs would then have ample time to populate all those countries where everyone would be living in happiness and equality.

After two hours of intense deliberation, it came time to vote. Verdict: Comrade Rappoport would not be obliged to terminate her pregnancy. She would not, however, be permitted to look after the child once it was born, for that would mean putting aside her political commitment. She would be allowed to decide for herself, and if she so desired in consultation with the child's father—Comrade Michał Gruda—what was to become of the child.

Said child made his appearance in the world on November 3, 1929, exactly ten days after the famous Black Tuesday crash, incontestable proof that capitalism had gone seriously astray.

My father, who defended my life with far greater virulence than my mother at the meeting where my future, or my absence of future, was discussed, did what every good Pole would do upon the birth of his first child: he ran out to share the news with all his friends, and celebrated the event each time with a little glass of vodka.

And so it was that years later, when I went to study in the USSR and used the occasion to try and obtain, at last, some papers attesting to the proof of my birth, I learned that I did not exist . . . at least, not under the name of Julian Gruda. The civil servant who handled my request informed me of the existence of a certain Ludwik Gruda, born in Moscow on November 3, 1929.

I called my parents in Warsaw. After they listened to my story, my mother came to the conclusion that, because they had oscillated for so long between the names of two famous Polish revolutionaries—Ludwik Warynski and Julian Marchlewski—my father, who had celebrated my birth all night with straight shots of vodka, must have got his heroes mixed up when he went to the public records office. And once he'd sobered up he must have forgotten which name he had written down on my declaration of birth. If I hadn't been in such a rush to have papers with my real name on them, I would surely have been amused by the anecdote, particularly as I found it quite hard to imagine my father drunk.

So that is how my life began, with a vote by the Polish Communist Party. In my favor. Fetuses of the world, unite!

Now that the outcome of the vote regarding my right to exist has been established, I suggest we travel back in time, to the year 1902, more than twenty-seven years before my birth, in order to meet Maria Demke, the lady who would never have the good fortune of becoming my grandmother.

PART ONE

CHAPTER 1
Life Before

Spring, 1902. Warsaw. Maria Demke was pregnant. She already had three daughters: Anna, Fruzia, and Karolka. The youngest was fourteen. After Karolka's birth, Maria's belly had little desire to grow round again. And then at the age of forty-one Maria discovered that a new life had come to curl up inside her.

At first, since it was winter, Maria wore an ample pelisse which enabled her to hide her condition. She was burdened by her growing womb, her swelling breasts, but it was not only her pregnancy that filled her with shame. Roughly one month before Maria learned of her state, Anna, her eldest, had informed her that she was expecting. Her eldest daughter: not even engaged, refusing to say a thing about the father's identity, with no intention of getting married, and perfectly happy with the state of events. When Maria realized that she too was pregnant, it was as if the sky had fallen on her head all over again. "What did I do to deserve these two misfortunes, one hard upon the other?" she asked a God who seemed endowed suddenly with a strange sense of humor. Gradually, however, she let herself go to this latest pregnancy, enjoying her renewed fertility; she was even delighted with this new opportunity to give her husband the son he had always dreamt of. She eventually came to view this new child as a gift from heaven, and every day she apologized to God for having berated Him.

One April morning, when her belly already seemed too heavy to her, Maria awoke before her husband. Soundlessly she slipped out of the sheets and went to prepare breakfast for the entire family. A first ray of sunshine filtered tentatively into the house through the kitchen window. Fruzia, the early riser among the Demke girls, went to join her mother. She was helping out, going to fetch water from the well, setting the table. When everything was ready, Maria asked her to go and wake her father. Then changed her mind: "Never mind, I'll go."

She didn't know why, when she had so much to do, she had insisted on going to wake her husband herself. She would often have the opportunity to praise the Lord, later on, for this gesture which saved her daughter from the painful discovery of her lifeless father.

Consequently, Mr. Demke never had the opportunity to meet his one and only son, the son who would become my father. During the last four months of her pregnancy, Maria wept every day, for she could not imagine life without her husband, the gentlest man she had ever met. Three months after Anna gave birth, Maria delivered her first son, in great pain. When the newborn child was laid on her belly and she heard, "Congratulations, Maria, it's a boy," she burst into tears. It tore her heart out, not to be able to share this happiness with her husband. And she went on crying, while nursing, bathing the baby, cooking, cleaning . . . until she had emptied herself of all the life left inside her, and had died of sorrow, four months after the birth of her son, the adorable little Emil.

It was Anna, the eldest Demke girl, who took the child into her home after Maria's death, and placed him on her left breast, while she placed Stach, her little bastard, on the right. And so Emil's childhood was spent between Anna, his sister-mother, and Stach, his brother-nephew . . . No father to speak of, whether temporary or regulation, in this quite ordinary life, with its everyday poverty, which was the lot of many of those who had come into Warsaw from the countryside to seek their fortune.

Anna was round and enveloping, and did everything she could so that her "little men" would lack for nothing. In the beginning, when she had to look after the two babies all day long, her sisters, who worked in a factory, gave her a bit of money to get along. Then Mr. Litynski, a widower who lived a few doors down and seemed to take kindly to his unmarried neighbor, told her about a friend who was in charge of distributing newspapers in the trams.

"Mr. Wolski is always on the lookout for new employees. It's not an ideal job for a woman like you, but at least it would enable you to clothe your boys in winter."

Anna liked the idea, and she already pictured herself crisscrossing Warsaw all day long, meeting lots of people. When Mr. Wolski saw this strong, smiling woman stride into his office, he did not hesitate for a second. A few days later Anna hired a young girl from the country to look after the boys, and she began her new trade.

Stach and Emil had a happy life, and it never occurred to them that things should be otherwise, that there should be a man at home, that Anna should not have to work all day long on her feet, running from one tram to the next. They ate when they were hungry, they were not cold in winter and, when they were sad, they could always curl up against Anna's two huge breasts, for they knew that there they would be safe from everything.

Until one day their life was turned upside down: Anna had a grave accident. She fell beneath a tram, and had to have her leg amputated. Emil, for all that he was only eleven years old, decided that henceforth it would be up to Stach and him to take care of Anna.

Very quickly it became clear that Emil was more resourceful than Stach, who had more of an artist's temperament. He managed to convince Mr. Litynski to speak to the newspaper vendor about him.

"I can distribute the papers in Anna's place."

"It's not as simple as all that. Look what happened to your mother, a woman who has her head on her shoulders, after all, and who knows how to get on in life. And you're only eleven."

"I can stay on my feet for a long time. And I have a good voice. And I have a cheerful face to boot, everyone has told me as much."

"I don't know. I can mention it to him, but he might not feel comfortable with the idea of having—"

"And does he feel comfortable with the idea that one of his former employees has only one leg and can't support her two children—one of whom, moreover, is her own brother?"

"There's a better solution, in my opinion. You should persuade your mother to come and live with me. We could make a nice family."

"All right, I'll tell her, but only if you promise me that you'll tell the newspaper gentleman about me and persuade him to meet me."

And so it was. Mr. Litynski persuaded his friend to meet Emil who, in turn, convinced him that he would be an excellent newspaper vendor. But Emil did not persuade Anna to go and live with Mr. Litynski; he didn't put much effort into fulfilling his part of the bargain, because he felt Anna didn't need a third man in her life.

Emil was eleven years old. With his resourcefulness and his cheerful face, he was earning more money than Fruzia and Karolka at the factory. He considered himself to be the man of the house, and he took the fate of his family very seriously, a family consisting of Anna, Stach, Fruzia, and Karolka. He did not merely sell newspapers, he also used his numerous trips on the tram to carry letters or packages from one end of town to the other.

1914. War broke out. The first of the world wars. As usual,

when the great European powers confronted one another, Poland was one of their favorite playing fields. In fact, Poland didn't even exist at that point in time, because in the eighteenth century the Prussians, the Austrians, and the Russians had turned it into a pretty little puzzle, and they had been having too much fun swapping bits back and forth. Even now the Russian and German armies were waging war on the territory that used to be Poland.

Newspapers sold out quickly in such hard times. In just under two hours Emil could earn what used to take him all day. Delivering parcels also brought in a lot of money, because people didn't leave their homes as readily, and Emil would even agree, for a slight additional sum, to transport parcels and letters after curfew.

One day a very important Russian man offered Emil a large sum of money to deliver a letter to his son, who was at the Russo-German front, to the west of Warsaw.

Emil, duly impressed by the fortune he had just been offered, wasted no time embarking on his mission. He took a few newspapers along with him, because he figured that the soldiers might want to read about the war they were risking their lives to fight. Bullets whistling overhead, little Emil made his way to the soldiers in their trenches. And while finding the recipient for his parcel proved more arduous than he expected, selling newspapers turned out to be extraordinarily easy.

That day Emil went home, opened the little leather bag he always wore slung across his shoulder, and spilled the contents onto the kitchen table. Anna looked at him gravely.

"Where did you get all that money?"

"I earned it, selling papers."

"Don't lie to me, please."

"I swear! It's because of the war, and with the front so nearby, people want to know what's going on, and the papers sell like hotcakes."

With an easy conscience—who could suspect a lie in what Emil had just told Anna?—the boy climbed into bed, his back to the wall, and set to dreaming about his day, the finest of his entire life, the fullest, the most important. "I'm a war hero," he thought.

For those few months while the Germans and the Russians were fighting outside Warsaw, Emil went every day to the trenches to sell papers to the Russian soldiers. Every time, he came back with his bag full to bursting; the soldiers were impressed with the little boy's courage, and sometimes gave him as much as ten times what the paper was worth. And he used the opportunity to learn Russian.

He could stay for hours in the trenches with the soldiers, waiting for a lull so that he could leave again, sometimes crawling, sometimes running as fast as he could. Emil liked the camaraderie that reigned among the soldiers, the solidarity shown by those young men who did not know whether they would ever see their homes or their families again. He loved to listen to them, to play dice with them, to smoke a butt or two. And they liked the little twelve-year-old, with his admirable courage and his bundle of anecdotes and jokes. Those few months would be etched on Emil's memory in a separate little frame: a sweet memory, with touches of fraternity, the curls of cigarette smoke, and stories told in confidence that were not really for his ears.

Not long after the war, Poland had to put together a new army, so Emil, now eighteen, joined up. "It's a good job, with a decent salary; I already know what war is like, and I'm not afraid. And anyway, we are bound to have a few years of peace ahead of us, after the long war we've just been through."

He was wrong. Already in 1920 he had to fight the Bolsheviks, who had managed to advance as far as Warsaw. On one side of the Vistula was the young army of the Second

Republic of Poland—inexperienced, badly organized and, above all, outnumbered. On the other side, thousands of Red Army soldiers were preparing to invade Warsaw. Then, unexpectedly, the Bolshevik troops withdrew and raised the siege on the town. In the history of Poland this episode is known as the "miracle on the Vistula," because so many Poles had prayed for Warsaw to remain Polish and free. Just the once wouldn't hurt: the Good Lord felt sorry for Poland and took her side.

During the siege Emil was fascinated by the enemy and their particular ideology. He had very animated discussions on the subject, because the other soldiers didn't like to see the pertinence of their war called into question. But Emil was not entirely convinced that everything about the enemy camped on the far side of the Vistula was evil. Since he spoke better Russian than most of the Polish soldiers, he was often called on to act as an interpreter with the prisoners of war. Sometimes he would go back to see them again after the interrogation was over and ask them about the situation in their country, and about the Bolshevik revolution. When the Soviets withdrew from Poland, Emil no longer knew what to think. He was deeply dismayed by the extreme poverty of the Polish peasants and workers. He convinced himself that there was a system where people were equal, and he was prepared to fight to see it triumph in Poland, at the cost of his life if need be. And he was increasingly convinced that only communism could lead to the liberation of the people and to class equality. So not long after he was demobilized, he set off for the office of the Polish Communist Youth, the KZMP, to request a membership card. Which he immediately took to show proudly to his friend Alek, one of the rare communist partisans he had met in the army: together they would celebrate this "historical moment" until the early hours of the morning. *Na zdrowie*, comrade!

Emil soon became a fervent member of the Communist

Youth. To earn a living, he unearthed a little job with a horti-culturist in the Praga quarter in Warsaw, but he then chose a more noble and revolutionary profession: metallurgist. He now officially belonged to the working class, and he devoted every spare moment to the struggle for the cause.

As the communist party was outlawed in Poland, Emil led a clandestine life: meetings, distribution of tracts, discussions with potential recruits, demonstrations, strikes, but also liter-ary evenings and the presentation of plays with a political fla-vor. He noticed that often when he left his house or his work there was someone following closely on his heels. He began taking more precautions. One day when he was speaking unguardedly with a few soldiers whom he was trying to per-suade to attend the next Communist Youth meeting, a man in an overcoat appeared out of nowhere and ordered him to go with him. Emil hesitated, noticed two men in the middle of the street attentively observing the scene, and complied. A few hours later, he was in prison.

Let's leave Emil Demke alone in his cell at Pawiak prison in Warsaw, because he would soon be meeting my mother, and it would be better for me to introduce her to you before I go thrusting her into my father's arms without warning.

My mother began her life as Guitele Rappoport. If I had set out to create a character with clearly recognizable Jewish ori-gins, I could not have chosen a better name. Rappoport is as Jewish a name as they come. And Guitele isn't exactly Chris-tian, either.

Guitele Rappoport—Gui to her friends and family—was born in Nowy Dwór, a little village located fifty kilometers from Warsaw, but the exact day and year of birth are unknown. According to her birth certificate she was born on March 3, 1903 (third day of the third month of the third year), but her father was waiting to have at least three children to declare before embarking on the journey into town, and so he chose birth dates at random for each child. My mother always made the most of this approximation to err on the side of youth and say that she was surely two or three years younger than what it said on her papers—until she turned eighty, and then from one day to the next she began to claim she'd been born at the turn of the century and was actually eighty-three. As she was in great condition for an eighty-year-old, people were stunned to find out her age.

Guitele's family was very pious. Her father was a kosher butcher, and a strict man, who took everything that had to do with religion very seriously. Guitele, like the three other children from her father's second marriage, had misguidedly chosen to be born a girl, so she was not given the opportunity to learn to read or write. At home they spoke Yiddish. Gui wanted to go to school, to speak Polish, to live a different life. The older she got, the more she hated her rigid father, and she dreamt of getting away.

At the age of ten she was sent to work at a dressmaker's. Although it was difficult work, Guitele was delighted to leave the house and meet people from other backgrounds. All the workers were Jewish, but most of them were from less pious families than her own. Gui listened to girls of fifteen or sixteen telling of their encounters with boys, or the parties they went to. She thought of Tobcia, her elder sister, who had never been allowed out in the evening and who had left home with the first man to give her a smile. And she began waiting for her turn.

Guitele was thirteen when she joined the seamstresses' union. The union leaders were her first heroes. She viewed them as models of uprightness, determination, and courage. Whenever there was a demonstration, she was in the front row, shouting louder than all the others; whenever there was a strike somewhere, she would be outside the gates every morning to stop the bosses going in, support the morale of the troops and ladle out hot soup. But in those days, that sort of militant behavior led straight to prison.

From the age of sixteen on, my mother was sent to prison several times over. If I'd had more of a chance to know what a mother's love is, I would surely have been very proud of her. She was a brave woman. A woman who created a new family for herself among the unions and, later on, in the Communist Party. A family for whom she was ready to make every sacrifice.

Prison played an important role in my mother's life. It is where she made her first goy friends and where she broke her ties with Judaism for good. To mark the break, she took a Polish name: Helena. She became known everywhere as little Lena. It was also in prison that she learned to speak Polish and then to read and write, and she developed a habit she would maintain all through life, that of doing regular gymnastics, which is surely why she was in such good shape right up to the time of her death. My mother spent just over four years in the Pawiak prison.

One gray morning in the spring of 1925 Helena was set free. And that same morning, under the same gray sky, a prison guard opened the gate and said goodbye to Emil Demke, who had just finished his sentence.

Emil saw a young woman sitting on a bench on Pawiak Square. Her face was vaguely familiar. Very timidly—she had just seen him leave the prison, he mustn't frighten her—he went up to her.

"Good morning, Miss. I don't mean to bother you, but I think I've seen you somewhere before . . . "

"Yes, yes, I remember you," answered the young woman with a strong Yiddish accent. "It was at a party at Magda Spychalska's. I think I've also seen you at a Party meeting. Maybe five years ago, before I went to prison."

Emil looked at her, stunned.

"Yes, I've just been released," she said, pointing to her suit-case.

I had just entered the realm of the possible.

The man who would become my father, who was scarcely taller than five foot two, was instantly charmed by this tiny little woman with her long braids. Oh, my mother's braids . . . She didn't cut them until the summer of 1940, shortly after France surrendered to the Germans. For years afterwards she would speak of them so nostalgically, as if, by cutting them, she had put an end to her youth, to a certain carefree time.

As neither one of them had anywhere to go, Emil invited Helena for a walk in the Bielany woods to see the trees in bloom. My father often told me of his meeting with my mother. This was how his story always ended: "And we went for a walk in the Bielany woods." Obviously, you might wonder what two people straight out of prison might do in a beautiful park on a gray day in spring . . . Since they were my future parents, I'd rather not venture an opinion on the subject.

From that moment on, Comrades Helena Rappoport and Emil Demke were comrades-in-arms. They were recognized for their commitment and their unshakeable faith in the communist model. To study the important role they would no doubt have to play in a post-revolutionary Poland, they were invited to spend a few months in Moscow, at a school run by the Comintern, to "perfect their communism." Emil Demke, as a militant communist, was once again being sought by the police, so the first thing he had to do was change his name. In the train that took him to Moscow he locked himself in the toilet holding a passport that had been duly filled out and bore all the necessary stamps and signatures, with a blank line for the first and last name. After careful reflection, he chose a name that corresponded to his peasant origins: Michał Gruda (in Polish *gruda* means "a hard, frozen clump of earth").

In Moscow, in the month of March, 1929, Helena

Rappoport discovered that she was pregnant. Before even telling Emil—whom she would never be able to call Michał—she informed Comrade Goldman, the secretary of her Party cell. Not batting an eyelash, Comrade Goldman gave her the name and address of a doctor who would be able to provide an easy solution to the problem. Lena went home, relieved. That evening, Emil came to fetch her, and they went out for a stroll through the Moscow streets, now covered in a thick blanket of snow.

"I have to discuss something with you. In fact, everything's been arranged, so you're not to worry, but I wanted you to know . . . I'm pregnant."

"What?"

"It's all right. I've already got an appointment with a doctor who practices abortions, there's nothing to worry about, everything will go fine."

"What are you talking about? Why do you want to have an abortion?"

"What do you mean, why? We can't possibly keep the child!"

"We could at least talk about it, don't you think? It's not a decision to be taken lightly."

"Look, Emil. When we go back to Poland, we'll have to go underground again. Can you picture us with a baby?"

"I understand, but I'd just like to have some time to think about it. It might be worthwhile to see if there isn't another solution, no? Besides, abortions are dangerous, I don't like the idea one bit."

"And anyway, from what I gathered from Comrade Goldman, the Party will never agree to let me keep the baby."

"I need to think about all this. When is your appointment?"

"In two weeks."

"Give me a day or two. Please, you think about it too, and we'll talk about it again, all right?"

"If you want."

That was my first victory.

The next day, Emil convinced Lena to raise the issue again with Comrade Goldman. Emil was present at the meeting, and refuted every one of the young woman's arguments. Which led, eventually, to the meeting on the 17th of March . . . But I already told you all about that.

We were in Moscow. I had just been born and registered at the public records office by a certain Michał Gruda, who was in a particularly joyful mood at the time.

The Party granted my parents permission to look after me until the end of their stay in the USSR. In the spring of 1930, the Comintern—the Communist International, the organization responsible for exporting Soviet communism to other countries—decreed that Comrade Helena Rappoport and Comrade Michał Gruda had completed their training, and they were sent back to Poland so that they could resume the bitter struggle on the path to revolution. The moment they arrived in Warsaw, they were reminded of their pledge not to keep little Julian. And thus I became Julian Kryda, the son of Fruzia and Hugo Kryda, who were the sister and brother-in-law of Michał Gruda, formerly my father.

I was not aware of these events that so discombobulated my life, because I was only ten months old when I landed with my aunt and uncle, not long after their youngest daughter had left home. Hugo and Fruzia happily agreed to take in a new child, this miniature version of Emil who reminded Fruzia of the difficult years of her youth, when she had found consolation for the loss of her mother by cuddling her beloved little brother.

My earliest memories date from this period in my life when I believed I was like everyone else, and I lived with the perfectly ordinary certainty that the people I called Papa and

Mama were indeed my mother and father; those years have remained etched on my memory.

There were occasional visits from a fat lady who smelled bad and spoke a language I couldn't understand. Every time they would tell me, "A nice lady is coming to see you this afternoon, she's going to bring you a lovely surprise." For starters, she wasn't nice, she always crushed me against her fat stomach and burst into tears, and then the presents she brought were anything but lovely: tasteless pancakes, sad, dark clothes that I refused to wear; I remember in particular a little round thing in black cloth that she wanted me to put on my head—it was a kippa, but I didn't know that at the time, and I never saw anyone wearing one—and Fruzia begged me to take it out whenever she knew the fat lady was coming. Much later I would find out that this was my maternal grandmother, Helena's mother, and she spoke only Yiddish. Her husband had said Kaddish—the prayer for the dead—for his daughter when he found out that she had had a child out of wedlock and, what was even worse, with a goy, so my grandmother came to see me in secret, under the pretext that she was visiting one of her sisters in Warsaw.

There was also a gang of kids there with whom I had a lot of fun. Fifteen or more boys, all under the age of ten, living in Colony 5, one of the eight housing co-operative complexes in ßoliborz set up by a left-wing association. Our colony was made up of a series of identical four-story white buildings, surrounding a big shady garden where there was an immense sandbox. From the age of three, I was one of the leaders of the younger group. When the big boys refused to include us in their games, I was often the one who came up with an idea for a game for the little ones, or for a prank. Hugo, who had daughters—daughters who, moreover, were well-behaved—took his role as father and educator very seriously. I wasn't a difficult or turbulent child, but I had a very, shall we say, inventive mind. So I spent many an hour at home being punished, and from time to time my bottom was subjected to a painful reminder of certain rules that I had failed to respect. I remember one particular spanking, one of the biggest I ever got, that I thought was clearly unjustified, because Hugo administered it in response to an idea that to me, for all that I was only five years old, seemed absolutely brilliant.

One summer's day, there were ten or more of us kids squabbling over some business to do with stolen chestnuts. Tadeusz was about to assume his role as referee when we heard someone in the street call out, "Photographs! Photographs for everyone! Memories, bargain price! Come and see me, you won't be disappointed!" I took off at a run out of the courtyard and through the door that gave onto Krasinski Street. A few minutes later I came back accompanied by a young man who was pulling all sorts of photographic equipment on a cart. "He'll take our photo and give it to us afterwards!"

These few words were enough to put an end to our quarrel. In compliance with the photographer's orders, we assembled in a group, some of us on our knees, others standing behind. It didn't take long for pandemonium to break out; no one listened to anyone else; the big boys pulled off the little boys' caps and threw them away, which made them burst into tears; and then there were those who absolutely had to be next to their best friend . . . Finally, the photographer shouted for everyone to shut up, and he warned, "I'm counting to ten, if you are still moving at the count of ten, I'll pack my things and I'll be gone. Do you understand?" A few minutes later, the session was over, and the photographer asked for his fee. Which I hadn't taken into consideration . . . All the children turned to look at me.

"It's my parents who wanted a photo, you'll have to go and see them for your fee. It's not hard to find: you see that door there, the one on the left? Go up to the fourth floor and to number 23. My papa is called Hugo, just say you're the photographer and he'll give you the money."

"Are you sure about that, kid?"

"Yes, don't worry, my dad is someone you can trust."

I don't know if, in my five-year-old mind, I really believed that I had just solved the problem. In fact, the problem was only finally solved with a dozen lashes of the belt and my being grounded for several days.

Parents are not always easy to understand: they have their own particular logic for determining what's good and what's evil. There was another matter that puzzled me concerning the approach that adults took to rearing their children.

I developed an acute political consciousness at a very early age. There was a lot of talk about politics at home for a start. Although they weren't committed communists, Hugo and Fruzia were sympathizers. I spent many a long evening with my ear glued to my bedroom door, or simply hiding under the table, listening to discussions between my parents and their friends. In Hugo's opinion people were always either too radical or too soft, so he loved getting his guests all worked up.

When Karolka, Fruzia's youngest sister, was arrested, there was talk of little else at home; she was a confirmed spinster who took part in every demonstration, in every militant action. We even went to visit her in prison once. Obviously, at my age, this was a big event. And Karolka's manner, both sad and proud at the same time, made a great impression on me, as if she were saying, "We will never give up." I was five years old at the time of that visit, and my aunt was a heroine to me, no doubt because I often heard Fruzia and Hugo praising her courage and tenacity. The communist gene was very strong in the family.

My first taste of class warfare dates to that period. One evening, Fruzia had already asked me at least five times to go to bed when there came a knock on the door. My parents were a bit surprised because they weren't expecting anyone, but they went to open the door. A giant wearing a policeman's uniform stood in the doorframe. Before he'd even said a word I was under the table. He spoke with Hugo and Fruzia for a long time; I think it was something to do with some thefts in our building. After a few minutes Fruzia had remembered her duties as a hostess and asked the policeman to have a seat at the kitchen table, and she offered him some tea.

I can clearly recall the policeman's legs beneath the flowered tablecloth, his perfectly polished black shoes. And the hatred that rose in me as I imagined those same feet kicking my Aunt Karolka as she lay in the street and growled, full of conviction, "We will never give up." And the feeling that it was time for me, too, to make a gesture on behalf of the poor and the oppressed. I looked at those two legs offered so candidly to me. I could see beneath the right trouser leg a muscular, hairy calf. Listening only to my courage, I crept closer, opened my mouth, and bit deep into that tough chunk of meat.

You can imagine the rest: the policeman leapt to his feet with a yell. Fruzia was aghast, the policeman caught me by the scruff of the neck and sent me flying to the other end of the kitchen, then Fruzia brought him a damp towel, apologizing profusely. Hugo watched the scene without batting an eyelid. Once things had calmed down, he looked at the policeman contritely and said, "I'm so sorry, Officer, my son loves to hide under the table and play dog. This is the first time he's ever bitten someone, I am truly sorry. He's in for one hell of a spanking once you're gone."

Once the policeman was gone, I tried to disappear beneath the blankets on my bed. Hugo came in the room.

"Papa, I wanted to punish him for what he did to Karolka. He's an enemy of communism!"

Long afterwards, from my room, I could still hear Hugo

and Fruzia's peals of laughter as they told each other the story. And I never got the spanking he'd promised the policeman was in store for me. I concluded that in life it is better to do what seems right without worrying about how your parents might react, because in any case, adults are unpredictable creatures.

Wh...hen I was Hugo and Fruzia's son, there was a couple who often came to visit us: Aunt Lena and Uncle Emil. They told me funny stories and brought me sweets, and Uncle Emil took me for walks in the Bielany woods where he taught me archery, how to climb trees, and how to do somersaults. He was a tiny man for an adult, and there were times when I thought he was really just a kid disguised as a grown-up.

One day Lena came without Emil. And the following time. And the time after that. I asked her why my uncle wasn't there, why he wasn't coming anymore, because I had to confess that even if I liked the sweets that Aunt Lena brought, I preferred playing with Uncle Emil by a long shot. She replied that he had left on a great journey, but as soon as he got back to Warsaw he would come and see me and bring me a nice present. "And he won't be too old to climb trees?" My question made the adults laugh, but they answered no, I mustn't worry about Emil's age, for he would always be a child at heart. This notion puzzled me. If you were a child at heart, would that still be enough to make an adult body work, even one as small as Emil's?

One day when I asked Lena for the umpteenth time when Uncle Emil would be coming back, and Lena once again said, "Soon, don't worry," I got that feeling you sometimes get when adults smile at you but their eyes aren't smiling, and then they stroke your hair: something "not for children" was going on. I didn't ask anything more as I could tell from her preoccupied manner that Aunt Lena wasn't going to say any more, even though I wasn't exactly born yesterday: I was six and a half years old. The only explanation I could come up with was that Uncle Emil must be dead, and I thought the grown-ups were being stupid to suppose I wasn't old enough to understand reality and accept it.

Not long after the beginning of this era of conspiracy, Hugo and Fruzia announced that they had something important to tell me.

"This year, for your summer vacation, you will be going on a long holiday."

"Where to?"

"First of all you'll take a train."

"A real train?"

"Yes . . . "

"Yay!"

"You'll be leaving next week, with Aunt Lena. You're going to Paris."

"I'm going to France?"

"Yes, my dear."

"And I'm going to see the Eiffel Tower?"

"Yes, you'll see the Eiffel Tower."

I was ecstatic. The Eiffel Tower! I'd heard so much about it, I'd even seen pictures in a book, I knew that from the top you could see all of Paris. Most of my friends were jealous, others thought I was making it up, that I was just going to the seaside or the mountains and I'd tell them any old thing when I got back.

"If you want us to believe you, you're going to have to bring back some proof," said Tadeusz, the biggest boy in the playground. "And not just some little souvenir that anyone could have brought you—we're not stupid."

"He'll have to show us a picture of himself in front of the Eiffel Tower."

"But the Eiffel Tower is too big to fit on a photo!"

"What are you talking about, Alek? Haven't you ever seen a photo of the Eiffel Tower? Where have you been all these years?"

"Well, I've seen the Eiffel Tower on photos, it's just that I've forgotten, it was when I was little."

"I'll show you a photo with me on it, that way you'll be obliged to believe me."

And I told myself that not only would I bring back a photo, I would also try to remember everything that happened, everything I saw during the holidays. When I got back, they would beg me time and time again to tell them about my trip to Paris.

One morning in July, 1936, I took the tram to the station with Hugo and Fruzia. I had two big suitcases that Fruzia had packed and repacked several times over the last few days. While I had been on cloud nine ever since they told me about my vacation in France, Fruzia, on the other hand, seemed really put out that we were going. A few minutes before we left the house she was still rushing around and around my room, getting clothes out of the suitcase and putting others in their place. Despite my happiness, it made me sad to see her like that. I tried to reassure her: "Don't worry, Mama, everything will be fine. I'll be good for Lena, nothing bad will happen to me." Which earned me a hug against Fruzia's breast so tight I nearly died of suffocation, not to mention the fact I almost drowned in a flood of tears, too.

That was the last time I ever called her Mama.

The train journey was endless. In the beginning I ran up and down, visiting all the carriages, talking with the conductors and the other passengers. I even made a few friends, but most of them got off the train before we even left Poland. It was nighttime when we reached Germany. I was intimidated by this country, by the voices on the loudspeakers in the stations, shouting in this harsh language I couldn't understand, and their red flags with swastikas hanging everywhere, and all the soldiers in their khaki uniforms. I knew these people were our enemies, the enemies of communists. I looked out the window of my carriage, and I was both fascinated and filled with hatred. All night long, in my berth, I was planning the revolution; I pictured myself walking through a big dusty city and setting fire to all the flags. I was riding a horse at the head of a huge crowd who followed me, shouting, "He's our leader! He bit the policeman!" Then a young woman who could have been Aunt Karolka wiped my face with a handkerchief.

"Julek, wake up, it's time to eat."

It took me a few seconds to figure out what was happening. Aunt Lena was leaning over me, caressing my hair. I could still hear shouting, but it was the loudspeakers in the station where our train had stopped, spluttering information for the passengers.

While we were eating, I noticed that Lena was looking at me oddly.

"Julek, my little Julek, I'd like to talk to you. I have something very important to tell you."

I was sure she was going to talk to me about the night before. I had the feeling I'd been shouting in my sleep, she must want to warn me about the Germans, maybe she was afraid I might bite one of them.

"You have to listen very carefully now. And if you're not sure you understand, if anything's not clear, don't hesitate to tell me."

"Okay."

"I know you love Fruzia and Hugo very much. I do too, they're very good people."

I had never noticed before how strange Aunt Lena could be.

"It's really hard to tell you this, but you must know the truth. Right. Fruzia and Hugo aren't your real parents. They have been taking care of you ever since you were little, and they have done a very good job. But you see, your real mother . . . I'm your real mother. And Uncle Emil is your real father. We couldn't look after you, because of the Party, because we were taking risks and we wanted to protect you. And we didn't want to give you up for adoption to strangers. Fruzia and Hugo very kindly offered to take you in. But now, for all sorts of reasons which I'll explain someday, you can't go on living there. Everything all right, so far? Do you understand?"

"Uh . . . yes."

"Good. So now we're going to France, and you're going to live with my sister Tobcia, who has a sweet little girl who's three years old. She'll be like a little sister for you. You'll be very happy with them."

My mind was racing. I could tell right away that what Lena was telling me was not true. And I understood perfectly what was going on: she was kidnapping me. In the book I'd been reading since the beginning of the trip (it was my first novel), a child is abducted by people who pretend to be his real parents. The child tells his kidnappers that he knows they are lying to him, and as a result he gets a thrashing. If I didn't want the same thing to happen to me, I absolutely had to pretend to believe her cock-and-bull story. Then I'd be able to work out a strategy to escape, and get back to Poland and to my real parents.

In Paris, Tobcia was waiting for us at the station. All you had to do was take one look at her, with her eyes protruding behind thick glasses, to know she was in cahoots with her sister (and maybe she wasn't even her real sister!). I smiled and said politely, "Hello, Aunt Tobcia. Yes, I had a nice trip. And you, how are you?" When I think back on it today, I am surprised that Lena didn't find my excessive politeness suspicious, because it wasn't my usual style.

We settled in at Tobcia's place with her husband Beniek, and Maggie, her "sweet little three-year-old," who of course turned out to be a real brat. A few days after our arrival we went to visit the Eiffel Tower. I was pleased but I couldn't make the most of that moment I'd been looking forward to so much, because my mind was bubbling with excitement. This outing might be my only chance to escape. In the street, I looked at every policeman we passed, and I tried to give them the sort of desperate smile that would incite them to ask Lena if they could speak to me in private. And then there was the language barrier . . . But I'd planned everything. I was going to ask for a sheet of paper and a pencil, and draw a child with his two parents, then a mean-looking woman sitting in a train next to a weeping child. It seemed clear enough to me. And even if they didn't get everything—I couldn't be sure that French policemen were any more intelligent than Polish ones—they at least ought to understand that I was in a difficult situation, and they'd ask a Polish interpreter for help. But French policemen were even stupider than I had imagined: not a single one came up to speak to me, not a single one gave me a puzzled look. I would have to resort to Plan B: find a way to get in touch with my parents.

When we arrived at the Eiffel Tower, for a few minutes I forgot the drama happening in my life, because I was overwhelmed with wonder at the sight of this enormous thing standing there before me. First we stood in line, with other families and a lot of children running all over the place. They were all speaking this language I couldn't understand. In spite of my situation, I really wanted to run and play with them. I looked at a little boy who was just behind us in the line and I made my ugliest face at him. Instead of laughing or of making an even more hideous face at me, he burst into tears and hid behind his mother's skirt. French kids were very disappointing.

Now it was our turn to go into the big metal box known as an elevator. The doors closed. And up we went! All the kids had their noses glued to the window and watched as the ground slipped farther and farther away, and the people below us got smaller and smaller. The elevator stopped on the first floor. Tobcia and Lena asked if I wanted to get out there. Out of the question, I wanted to get to the top as quickly as we could. On the second floor, we had to leave the elevator to take another one . . . which was under repair. Lena informed me in a sorrowful tone that we couldn't go any higher, but if we liked, we could come back another day, once the second elevator was repaired. She's a funny one! I noticed some other kids going with their parents up some stairs to the third floor, so I rushed off toward the stairway and started to squeeze past the people who were already on the stairs so that Lena couldn't catch me.

And then there I was, all the way at the top! I looked down below me: the people were tiny! Little ants! No, maybe not quite . . . mice? I had to find precise words for my descriptions, to be able to tell my friends everything once I got back to

Warsaw. Warsaw . . . I absolutely had to make the most of these few minutes of freedom to find a way to get home.

When Lena and Tobcia, who had decided to follow me up the stairs, eventually arrived, I already had my plan. I asked for some coins so I could play this little game in a machine that consisted of trying to pick up objects or candy by manipulating a little crane. If you managed to catch something, it was yours. Lena agreed. It was a very hard game, but I was determined: my life depended on it. On the fourth try, I fished out a red cigarette lighter. Perfect!

Back at the house, after asking Tobcia for some paper and string, I shut myself in the room that I shared with my "cousin" Maggie. Maggie tried to steal the lighter from me, insisted on drawing on my sheet of paper, and generally got on my nerves. I gave her a little pinch on the shoulder and she left the room, howling. Good riddance. It took me a long time but I managed to make a package that looked very classy. As I hardly knew how to write, I resigned myself to asking Lena to help me with the letter to go with my package. I had to be very subtle so I wouldn't arouse her suspicions. I thought for a long time, and started the message over in my head a hundred times. This was what I came up with that seemed closest to perfection, and finally I dictated it to Lena, acting nonchalant:

"Dear Papa,
"I'm in Paris now with Lena and her sister Tobcia. We have just visited the Eiffel Tower. I have a little present for you that I fished on the third floor of the tower. It's so you can light your pipe. I think we're going to be staying here for a long time. I really want to see you and Mama again soon.
Julek."

I didn't write "Aunt Lena," although normally that's what I called her. There was also the indication of where we were (with Tobcia) and the penultimate, and very important, sentence in the letter, which should make Hugo understand that something abnormal was going on.

Lena wrote the letter. I put it in the envelope, and she sealed it.

"You have to put the address on the envelope."

"Of course, darling."

"And will you mail my present soon? I'd like him to get it before his birthday."

"Yes, of course. I have a few errands to run tomorrow, so I'll go to the post office while I'm at it."

But of course she didn't go to the post office, as I would find out many years later. Why not? Wasn't it because she had seen through my little game? Of course not, I think I'd been perfectly convincing in my role. The reason was much simpler, and it was a sad one. The Party had asked her not to have any more contact with my father's family, including Hugo and Fruzia.

It must now be time to explain the reasons behind this "kidnapping" and my departure for France.

Now for the true story behind my abduction by my aunt who, I believed, was pretending to be my mother, but who in fact had carried me in her womb . . .

Emil Demke, now known as Michał Gruda, was appointed the officer for propaganda of the Polish Communist Party (KPP) in the Polish army. Through meetings, tracts, and assemblies, his job was to persuade as many soldiers as possible to join the Party. His activities meant that the police were after him. Since the Party didn't want to lose this very devoted member, and they were afraid he would be arrested again, they sent Michał to Moscow, where there were a lot of Polish communists biding their time in the hopes of being forgotten by the Polish authorities.

No sooner had he arrived in Moscow than Michał was sent on to Kiev, where he would be in charge of propaganda for the Poles who lived in Ukraine. There he joined other Poles who were active on the town committee. He toured factories where he was sent to discuss politics with the Polish workers, the majority of whom felt they'd gotten a raw deal from the communist regime. He explained, ever so fervently, the benefits of communism, thanks to which they had the right to a decent life, even just as simple factory workers. Michał also did some casual journalism and wrote for *Sierp* (*The Sickle*), a paper published by the Polish communist party.

In 1934, once he'd imprisoned and executed the communists who opposed him, mainly Trotskyites, Joseph Stalin began to go after the communists who believed in him. And the first pro-Stalin communists to be arrested were . . . the Polish communists in Kiev. All those people who, like my father, were in the USSR because of their immense faith in the communist doctrine and their boundless admiration for Comrade Stalin. The Kiev Poles working for the organization of the Bolshevik Party were all arrested for high treason. My father was in the wrong place at the wrong time.

As Stalin was still eager to do things by the book, every prisoner was entitled to his or her own personalized bill of indictment. Michał Gruda was accused of being an agent in the pay of Piłsudski (the leader of Poland, at the time). What proof was there of his betrayal?

"In 1933, did Comrade Gruda not foment a strike at a cardboard factory? The strike was a failure. Is it good for our cause that a strike should end in such a way? Of course not. And who stood to gain from this failed strike? The great capitalist powers, of course. It is patently clear that Comrade Michał Gruda is working against us, that he is an enemy of the people and, therefore, an enemy of communism."

All of this was so obvious, so clear . . . but wasn't all.

"Is it not true that capitalists and other imperialists are determined to see the fall of the USSR, the homeland of the working class? Therefore, should we not display the greatest vigilance with regard to agents who are working for the destruction of this world of ours, where social inequalities no longer exist? It is always possible, even desirable, to increase one's level of vigilance, is that not so? Therefore, if you, Comrade Michał Gruda, known for your great devotion to the cause, confess to being a traitor in the pay of the enemy, will that not incite other comrades to be even more vigilant? Then sign at the bottom of the bill of indictment, just there."

My father could not refute the logic behind their reasoning, and he was not even offended by the extreme manipulation underlying it. But he refused to place his signature at the bottom of a document that was nothing but a string of lies.

And this went on for a long time. They tried everything to make him crack. Everything, except physical torture. Which was only added to their arsenal after 1937. My father was fortunate to have been arrested at a time when they still drew the line at mental torture.

Michał shared a cell with thirty or more prisoners. From time to time a guard would come into the cell in the middle of the night with a paper in his hand and go up to each prisoner and ask, "Family name?" The prisoner would give his name. "No, that's not it." And he'd try the same game with the next prisoner, until eventually he said to one of them, "Yes, you're the one. Follow me." The prisoner would leave the cell and never come back.

One day it was my father's turn to follow the guard. "Shall I take my things?" "As you like, it won't change anything." They took him out to a truck where there were twelve soldiers with rifles. The truck started up. The journey was spent in complete silence, and it seemed endless. Finally the truck came to a halt in the middle of a forest. A soldier told the prisoner to get out, then he was blindfolded and tied to a tree. Michał could hear footsteps, and the sound of rifles being cocked. He was afraid, but not sad. In his mind there was a great emptiness. Someone shouted, "At the enemy of the homeland, FIRE!"

Then nothing. Not a sound, not a word. He was untied and made to climb back into the truck. The same route, still in silence, only this time his eyes were covered, no one had bothered to remove his blindfold. Back at the prison he was led straight to the director's office.

"Comrade Michał Gruda! Sit over there in that chair. A little vodka? A cigarette? Annushka will bring us some *zakuski*, you must be dying of hunger." Michał drank a little vodka, ate something, smoked a cigarette, had some more vodka. He felt his blood gradually warming, his legs going soft. He wondered if any of this was real.

"And now we are going to finish dealing with your case once and for all. Right, here are your papers, just sign there, Comrade, because next time we take you out to the woods, things won't end the same way . . . "

But none of these strategies worked. Most of the Kiev Poles had signed. And they had been shot. My father's stubbornness saved his life, and earned him a conviction of three years in the gulag in Siberia . . . where he stayed for six years. Why did they need a signature at the bottom of a fake document in order to execute people? Who knows. Stalin's mind and his logic remain too complicated for me.

When the Polish Communist Party found out about the accusation against my father and his deportation to Siberia, the leaders went to see my mother to tell her that her son mustn't stay with the Krydas, because they belonged to the same family as that traitor—otherwise she herself would be shown the door and asked to leave the Party. As she could not imagine looking after me or leaving the Party, she asked her sister Tobcia in Paris to take me in.

That was the true story behind my presence in a country where I couldn't speak the language, where I sat in a girl's room, my eyes closed, hoping that my letter and a lighter I'd won at the Eiffel Tower would manage to arouse Hugo and Fruzia's suspicions.

CHAPTER 6
Toward a New Life

One morning after breakfast, Lena said, "We're going for a drive in a car today. Then we'll go and visit a fantastic place where there are lots of children your age. You'll be able to play with them all you want."

I definitely wanted to go for a drive in the car.

"And the children, are they all French?"

"Yes, don't worry, they will play with you even if you don't speak the same language."

That wasn't really what bothered me, it was just that my one attempt to approach a French kid had ended in failure. So I figured I would avoid making faces, maybe it was something they were unfamiliar with here, and I'd wait, rather, for them to decide what to play—I was the foreigner, after all, so it was normal that I make the effort to adapt.

So there I was at the "fantastic place with lots of children," full of good intentions. Lena, Tobcia and I went through a park leading to a big white building with ochre shutters. While we were walking in the courtyard, I could hear children shouting, and on a dirt playground on the side of the building I saw some boys and girls playing ball. I wondered if they'd forced the boys to play with the girls. If that was the case, I felt sorry for them. I also saw two boys about my age perched at the top of a tall tree in the park. When we walked by, they tried to hide. Maybe you weren't allowed to climb trees in this place? And yet there were some huge ones, with very inviting branches that began at just the right height for a kid my size. I stayed on the alert: if the two women with me took their eyes off me, I would find a tree and climb up and hide in it, quickly. Maybe I could shake off my kidnappers like that.

Lena and Tobcia headed for the front door of the building. We went in. A lady came to speak to us, went away again, then came back with a man. He spoke with Tobcia for a long time, because she was the only one of us who could speak French. From time to time he would glance at me and nod his head. After what seemed like a very long time—I was nervous at the prospect of my imminent escape—the man came over to me, said something I couldn't understand, took me by the hand and made some gestures, as if he were asking me to say good-bye to Lena and Tobcia. Lena, who hadn't said a thing since we entered the park, came closer:

"My darling, you seemed so bored at Tobcia's, so we decided to bring you here so you can make some friends. I'll come and see you often, don't worry. I'll come next week and bring you some more clothes."

For the first time I noticed a little suitcase that Lena must have been carrying since we left Tobcia's apartment. I didn't know what to make of the situation. Was the man one of Lena's accomplices? Should I try to escape? Or was I rid at last of the woman who had kidnapped me? I concluded that she must be leaving me here so that Hugo and Fruzia wouldn't know where to find me.

"And how long will I be here?"

"Well, at least until the end of the summer, and after that we'll see. If you like it here, perhaps you can stay for the school year."

Tobcia and Lena kissed me and left. And there I was among all those people I couldn't understand and who couldn't understand me. The man was still holding my hand and now he led me to a dormitory. He showed me one of the beds in a corner of the room, and put my suitcase down on it. He gave me a smile and said something that seemed to end with a question mark. I shook my head. I had no idea what he had said, but since there was nothing I wanted, I answered in the negative. He ruffled my hair, smiled, and went away.

I was all alone in the big dormitory. I should have been happy: I was free and I could devote myself actively to finding a way to contact Hugo and go back to Poland. But I had a lump in my throat and my eyes were stinging.

CHAPTER 7
L'Avenir Social

S o there I was, settled in at L'Avenir Social (AS for friends and acquaintances), an orphanage which took in not only orphans but also children from impoverished families, or whose parents were in prison for political reasons, and the children of communist militants from a number of countries. The AS was run by the CGT, the Communist trade union. The philosophy of the place was founded above all on respect for the children, who were allowed to express themselves freely, and who were being taught to think for themselves. But I would only find all that out much later on.

The first striking moment of my stay at L'Avenir Social was my meeting with Arnold, one of the instructors, whose principal qualities, or at least those I noticed right from the start, were that he was of Polish origin and could speak my language. He was a tall, slightly stooped fellow with a piercing but gentle gaze, a long face, chestnut hair in a crew cut and—a characteristic that fascinated all the children—three fingers, two fused together, on his left hand. He had a natural joy about him, and took everything with a sense of humor. He was the favorite instructor of most of the children, and this earned him the nickname "My Pal." Thanks to him, if I had something important to say, it was possible to do so. I had my own personal interpreter. I could chat with him, listen to his stories, and ask him questions. I was waiting to get to know him better, all the same, before deciding whether I could trust him enough to tell him about my abduction. He was also the only person there who called me Julek, the diminutive of Julian in Polish—to everyone else, my name was Jules Kryda—and I took comfort in hearing my old name from time to time.

One piece of good news: there were some French children who actually were fun. I'd just been unlucky on my visit to the Eiffel Tower. Some of them even had a repertory of nasty faces every bit as good as my own. With the other "orphans" communication was not a problem: they spoke to me in French and I answered in Polish. We probably lost a certain amount of subtlety, but it was enough to be able to play dodgeball or cops and robbers.

Only a few days after my arrival, there was an unpleasant incident. We were standing in a line outside the refectory, waiting for the doors to open for the midday meal. Behind me, I heard a very shrill and stupid laugh. I turned around, and saw a skinny little boy with a turned up nose and ears that stuck out. He was looking at me, still laughing. He seemed to be making fun of me. I immediately disliked his stuffed owl manner. Obeying only my pride, I jumped on him, and with all my strength, fists clenched tight, I hit his little freckled nose. After his initial surprise he grabbed me by the neck and tried to strangle me. I couldn't see anymore, couldn't hear, I was biting and kicking in every direction. It took two adults to pull us apart and end the scuffle. I had trouble getting my breath back, and I saw that my hands were bleeding. My opponent was sitting on the floor, his head thrown back, and a woman was holding a handkerchief firmly over his nose. Well, his little turned up nose wasn't so solid after all, I thought, wiping my hands.

As a punishment, I had to spend the entire meal standing in a corner of the refectory with my back to everyone. The owl got off scot-free. All through my punishment I was fuming. I could understand that what I'd done might warrant a sanction, but I found it hard to accept the fact that the kid who'd made fun of me and almost strangled me had gotten off so lightly.

After the meal I was released from my humiliating position. I left the refectory, not looking at anyone, and went to sit on my bed. I was disheartened: I still didn't know whether I'd manage to get back to Poland, and I thought my stay here had gotten off to a very bad start. That afternoon, I realized that the other children were smiling at me more often than usual, and now and again they gave me a wink or a pat on the back. It was always discreet, when there were no adults around. I began to suspect that the pretentious little brat I'd given a thrashing to wasn't one of the most popular kids around.

The day after my fight, while I was feeding the rabbits in the farmyard at the far end of the park, I saw Arnold's tall form coming toward me.

"*Jak tu idzie?*"

"*Dobrze.*"

For those of you who don't speak Polish, let me start again, with a free translation.

"How are you doing?"

"I'm okay."

"I see you've become acquainted with our little long-eared residents. Which one do you like best?"

"The gray and white one. It's as if he can see me coming from a distance, and he's always happy to see me."

"His name is Smartie, but he isn't really all that smart. I heard about a little misadventure you had. What happened, exactly?"

I hesitated.

"Don't you want to talk about it?"

"No."

"I know you can't defend yourself with words yet. But if there's anything that makes you angry, anything hurtful about the way the other children behave, I'd like you to come and speak to me about it first before lashing out like a lunatic."

"I'm not a tattletale."

"No, of course not . . . Which is all to your credit. And I don't want you to squeal on anyone; I just want you to come and see me so I can help you communicate with the other kids. For a start, do you know who he is, this Roland you attacked?"

"No."

"You know Henri, the director, the one who greeted you when you first got here? Well, it's his son."

The owl was the director's son! In that case, my stay really was off to a very bad start. And suddenly I had something like a flash of insight, and it all became perfectly clear: Henri, of course, was bound to be in cahoots with Lena and Tobcia, otherwise he would have kicked me out after my little squabble with his beloved little boy. But since the conspiracy was more important than anything, he had no choice . . . So I really was in a pickle.

One week later, everything was in an uproar at L'Avenir Social. All the suitcases were out on the beds, the oldest kids packing their own, and the littler ones getting help from the instructors. I had to borrow clothes from other kids because Lena still hadn't had time to come and see me. Thanks to Arnold I knew we were going on vacation to an island, a place called the Île de Ré. I was really glad because I'd see the ocean for the first time. And now I had a friend, too: Bernard, a shy boy who was a little younger than me, he must have been five or so. We promised we would sit together on the train. I knew a few words of French now, the most obvious ones like yes, no, thank you, hello, goodbye, please, eat, drink, and of course, *merde*. And others, too, to describe my life at L'Avenir Social: rabbit, dog, friend, apple, pear, tree, marble, ball, play, run, and the newest one: vacation—but that wasn't hard, because it was almost the same in Polish, *wakacje*. The kids made fun of the way I pronounced the *r*s, rolling them. I practiced really hard with Bernard, trying to say *poire* the way the other kids did, but for the time being it sounded more like I was clearing my throat.

I loved our vacation on the Île de Ré, because of the ocean, but above all because of the huge green lizards I played with the whole time I was there. I would place one over my shoulder then head off for a walk along the beach. I made my decision: later on in life I would be an animal trainer. I also made friends with a fluffy little white dog called Bibi. He followed me everywhere and would run up to me the moment I called him. Since I spoke to him in Polish, and he listened very attentively, the other children came to the conclusion that I spoke dog language. Bernard, given his status as my best friend, even wanted me to teach him a few words of "dog." I decided not to tell them the truth. After all, it was true that Bibi did seem to understand everything I said to him. Maybe Polish really is a language with which to communicate with dogs. Even Roland the owl was dazzled by my talents, and when he saw me deep in conversation with Bibi, he would watch, looking very impressed. This vacation was the last time in my life that I was able to make the most of my status as a foreigner, because by the time we returned to the orphanage everyone knew that I could understand what they said in French. And that I could communicate in French.

I had a new friend at L'Avenir Social, a girl. Her name was Geneviève. She was one of the instructors. She was funny and kind, but she also knew how to be strict and demanding. Every time she saw me she would exclaim, "Look at his periwinkle eyes! He's so sweet!" There was a rumor going around that she and Arnold were in love. It was Roger who was behind the rumor—Roger Binet, to whom we'd given the nickname Robinet (which means water faucet in French, and much later I'd be sorry I'd called him that so often, just to annoy him). I was no expert on love, but it was true that you could often see them whispering together, maybe that was how you could tell when people were in love.

It was fun talking to Geneviève. For a grown-up she listened to me very attentively. One day she told me that "my mother" would be coming to visit later that day. She was surprised when I showed no enthusiasm.

"I know this is the first time she's coming to see you, but she's been very busy since she brought you here. She must be very eager to see you again."

"She's not even my mother."

"What do you mean?"

Well, it was now or never. I'd finally found the right person to confide in, and my French was good enough. So in I went.

"She kidnapped me from my real parents, Hugo and Fruzia Kryda, in Warsaw. She said she was my mother, but I know that was just a trick so that I wouldn't run away during the trip. I want to go home to my real parents in Warsaw. I miss them a lot."

Geneviève was not the sort to say anything just to break the silence, so she looked at me without saying a word. Her eyes went moist, her cheeks red. I waited for a long time.

"Jules, my little Jules . . . I beg you to believe me, Lena is your real mother . . . She had no choice, when you were a baby, other than to leave you with those people who looked after you as if they were your parents. And she had no choice, later on, but to take you away from them again. She has done it all for your own good . . . You have to believe me."

I couldn't speak.

"I would like so much to convince you. One day you will see them again, those people who brought you up, but for now it's better for you to stay here, my sweet. Lena loves you very much, you know. Be nice to her, please. You will, won't you?"

I still didn't speak.

"Think about it then, a little, all right? I have no reason to lie to you, you know that, don't you? Think about it and we'll talk again after your mother's visit. Come on, it's time to eat, go and join your friends at the refectory."

I wasn't hungry. I didn't feel like joining anyone. I went out into the park and I walked, somewhat aimlessly, until I reached the rabbit hutches. I was cold and it felt good. Smartie came over to me, all happy, but I had nothing to give him. All I had for him was my own story, and it didn't make sense to me anymore. He looked at me with big sad eyes. He wouldn't want to be in my shoes. I knew that Geneviève hadn't been lying to me. I could tell. She would never have done such a thing. But for all that, it didn't necessarily mean that Lena's story was true; Tobcia surely told them this version when she brought me here, and no one had any reason to question it. That was my one remaining hope. And yet for some reason I felt that Geneviève knew a lot more about my life than she was letting on—and about Lena's. Smartie nudged his little nose against my hand, as if to say he agreed. But why would Hugo and Fruzia have lied to me? I didn't feel like seeing Lena. I wanted to run away, and go far, far away.

"Julek, come on, wake up."

Arnold was speaking to me. I didn't understand why he had come to wake me up in the middle of the night.

"Your mommy is waiting for you in the lounge. She doesn't have a lot of time."

It took me a few minutes to get my wits about me. I was lying among the dead leaves just next to the rabbit hutches. There was a pebble under my left buttock and it hurt. I stood up and followed Arnold, docilely; I hadn't quite emerged from my dream. I had been playing with my friends in Warsaw. Each of us had a big black box which we used as a house, with only one little window drawn onto one of the walls. It was very small and dark inside, but I loved it there, and I no longer existed, for anyone.

"*Julek! Mój kochany! Opowiec mi, jak tu ci idzie?*"

"I'm fine."

I didn't have much to tell her. She asked how my French was coming along. I told her, *Bien*. In French. She asked me whether Arnold was still speaking to me in Polish so that I wouldn't forget my language; I said yes. She asked me whether I'd made friends, whether I was having fun, and whether I was eating well. *Oui, oui, oui*. And so on. Then she told me that she had been on vacation in the mountains, where she did a lot of walking, and she was very tired, but the scenery was beautiful. Just before she left she took a little box out of her handbag. Inside there were pink bonbons and white bonbons, shaped like eggs. And she left me a suitcase with clothes and asked me if there was anything I needed. *Non*. She kissed me hard on both cheeks and left.

I had lied to her. Ever since I'd started to get on in French, Arnold had stopped speaking to me in Polish. And I was very grateful to him. I was ashamed of that language that reminded me of Lena and made me different from the others. And now I had yet another reason not to speak Polish: I was beginning to understand that the only people for whom I'd want to continue speaking Polish—Hugo and Fruzia—had betrayed me.

All through the years I spent in France, the only thing I remembered of my mother tongue were the few words I taught the children not long after I arrived at L'Avenir Social, when they asked to learn to speak dog language. Four little nothing words: *tak, nie, gówno* and *krolik*. Translation: yes, no, shit, and rabbit. I was too young when I arrived to teach them anything more vulgar.

In the weeks that followed my meeting with Lena and my discussion with Geneviève, the truth quietly worked its way into my mind. Before long the theory of a conspiracy would be consigned to the deepest recesses of my memory. In any event, my new life was with the other children at L'Avenir Social, I was finding it harder and harder to understand Polish, and I didn't want to go back to Hugo and Fruzia anymore. Even though, at night, I often dreamt about Fruzia, and I could feel her warmth, and her fingers stroking my hair.

Several months went by before my mother came back to see me, in the summer of 1937. By then I was a regular boy at L'Avenir Social, with my friends, my habits, my world—in short, my life. I was no longer one of the little boys—affectionately known as the brats—because I was seven-and-a-half years old. When one morning Geneviève came to tell me that Lena was there to visit me, my initial reaction was to refuse to see her. The fact was, after several rainy days the weather was fine again, and we Cowboys would at last be able to take our revenge upon the Indians, who had won the two previous wars. Geneviève had to search for a long time before she found me, because I was tucked away inside my favorite hiding place, ready to attempt an ambush. But she had a loud voice, and after pretending not to hear her repeated calls of, "Jules, where are you?" I finally relented and turned myself in, making sure no one saw me climbing out of my lair. But when she broke the news, I replied that my mother had to let me know in advance when she was coming, because I had other things to do—"And who does she think she is?" This last sentence was, obviously, a grave mistake from a strategic point of view, and I knew it even before Geneviève replied, very calmly, "Your mother?" then went on to add, "And she wants to take you to the movies. But if you don't feel like it, I'll tell her to forget about it." Well, the movies . . . and besides, at the movies you didn't have to talk.

It was disconcerting to see Lena again. First of all, she

came in, all happy, gave me a big hug, and then began talking very quickly . . . in a language I didn't know. To my great surprise, I could no longer understand Polish. At all. I didn't recognize a single word pouring from my mother's lips. Although one word did stand out in the middle of all the gibberish: *Tarzan*. That must be the film she wanted to take me to see. I was astonished to find out that my mother had such good taste in movies, but I didn't complain, because it was excellent news.

Off we went on the bus. I told my mother about my friends, our games, the newborn baby rabbits . . . She always answered saying, "*Oui, oui*," or "Hmm." In the beginning I thought it was strange: after all the time she had been in France, my mother must surely speak French. I gave her the benefit of the doubt, and told myself she was probably embarrassed because of her accent.

After the movies, we stopped to eat ice cream. I was excited and completely swept up by the movie, by this Tarzan who lived in the jungle with his friends the apes. I had trouble sitting still and eating calmly. I wanted to talk about the film.

"I wish I could make Tarzan's jungle cry."

I made a first attempt. Which left something to be desired.

"Yep, I'll have to practice."

Lena laughed.

"I want to go to the jungle. Do you know where they have monkeys, which country?"

"Yes, yes . . . "

"So where is it?"

"Hmm . . . "

"I asked you, where do they have monkeys, which countries!"

"Oh, okay!"

"Rats, I don't believe it!"

I did a fairly successful imitation of a monkey, shrieking and scratching under my armpits.

"Where do they have monkeys?"

This time I spoke very loudly, articulating and exaggerating every syllable, as if I were addressing a half deaf old woman.

"Hmm . . . I do not know."

I didn't even feel like talking about Tarzan anymore. I finished my ice cream in a hurry and stood up. On the way home, we hardly spoke. I put my nose to the window in the bus and watched the countryside go by, and I pictured myself running through the tall grasses with my friends the apes, climbing the tallest trees, swinging from branch to branch as I clung to the hanging vines.

When we got to the orphanage, the children were all lined up outside with packs on their backs, as if they were getting ready to go on an expedition. As soon as we were through the gates, I took off at a run. I was afraid I was too late and was going to miss something. Arnold stopped me.

"Hey! Where are you going, running like that?"

"Well, I don't know, where are you going?"

"We're going swimming in the canal. If you hurry and fetch your swimsuit and a towel you can come with us. And your mother, too, if she wants."

"I'll let you ask her."

I ran up the steps four at a time, into the dormitory, rummaged through my clothing, took out a pair of underwear that was cleaner than the others, grabbed my towel, trying to fold it the way the others did, didn't manage, never mind, it didn't matter; I ran back down the stairs, and not even five minutes later I was lined up with the other children.

To get to the canal, we had to take the main road that led from L'Avenir Social to the village of Villette-aux-Aulnes. We were walking in file two by two, like good little soldiers, with one instructor in the front and two bringing up the rear. No running off to the side would be tolerated, that we knew, and apart from Fabrice, who was a hothead and kept dodging off to climb fences outside the houses we passed, no one left their place in the line. From time to time one of the little ones would get a clout, or someone would shout something stupid to make the others laugh, or one of the big kids would say, "Hi, gorgeous," to a girl passing in the street, but we knew we had better behave if we didn't want to be excluded from the excursion and be forced to stay all alone at L'Avenir Social under Henri's surveillance.

We walked across a field belonging to the Dumoutiers. They were nice people; they had a very old granny you had to lead home whenever you found her wandering around the field. She always smiled. Whenever she saw us, she would hurry over, usually to the youngest girl, and she would pinch her cheeks and scold her for some reason known only to her.

After the field, a narrow little path led through the woods, and then down the slope to the canal. As soon as we got there, everybody rushed to put on their swimsuit, the boys in plain sight, the girls using their towels as a screen. Those who knew how to swim rushed into the water, splashing about as much as they could. I wasn't one of them. Never mind, it was fun by the canal all the same, but when it was fine weather and hot like it was that day, I would have given my entire collection of pebbles to be able to jump into the water and swim with the others. Arnold took me discreetly by the elbow and led me over to Lena: "Spend some time with your mother, she has to go back to Paris soon." Lena said something to him and seemed to be scolding with her index finger, surely a reproach for having lapsed in his role as guardian of my Polish. She should have just left me in Poland if she wanted me to speak Polish. It served no purpose here.

She went on speaking to me in Polish, and I would reply in French, while my mother went, "*Oui, oui.*" Same old refrain.

"Do you know how to swim?"

"*Oui, oui . . .* "

"Well, why don't you go into the water?"

"Hmm . . . I do not know."

If she knew how to swim, there was no reason for her to go on sitting next to me carrying on this dialogue of the deaf. I stood up, made a gesture to Lena to do like me, and . . . I shoved her in the water.

Well. The truth was that she didn't know how to swim, not even a smidgin. Lena's fall into the water caused quite a commotion. First of all she started screaming, then when she was in the water, she began waving her arms in distress and splashing everywhere. Then people ran towards us, some of them yelling at me, and others shouting contradictory instructions; two or three girls burst into tears, and finally Arnold, the only one who kept his wits in all the commotion, jumped into the water, grabbed hold of my mother and dragged her over to the ladder to get her out of there.

I sat back down on my towel and waited for whatever might happen next, which didn't take long. Arnold came up to me.

"Would you care to explain to me what happened?"

"Well, I asked her if she knew how to swim, she said yes. How was I to know she would answer any old thing!"

"She didn't answer any old thing, she surely misunderstood your question, you must have noticed that her French is not very good."

"Well she shouldn't answer, if she doesn't understand! If she answers, I can't—"

"All right, all right, I know you didn't mean her any harm. But it is not a very smart idea to push someone in the canal, even if they do know how to swim. You do understand, don't you, that Lena could have drowned? You're going to have some time to give some serious thought to all that."

"Time to give some serious thought" meant three whole

days where I was not allowed to take part in any activities. I could only go out and sit on the "thinking chair" located behind the building of L'Avenir Social. And it was from this humiliating position that I heard the Cowboys' cries of victory when they won their first big battle, without me.

As a name for an orphanage, L'Avenir Social must sound a bit pompous. But it wasn't just to show off, our establishment was an orphanage for workers, its allegiance was communist, and it advocated the right to universal education. All our instructors sincerely wanted to turn us into adults capable of autonomous reflection, committed to society. We learned to read and write at the village school; at the AS, the instructors made sure to teach us everything else: an appreciation of nature and history, how to show respect, thoughtfulness, compassion, and helpfulness, and how to live with others . . . There was also a political side to our education, and in my case this began with the Spanish Civil War.

One day when we were playing in the yard, Arnold called to us in his loud voice to gather round. There were a dozen or so of us. He squatted down, and in the dirt on the ground he made a big drawing.

"You've already heard about what's going on in Spain. Now I want to explain it all to you in detail. Look at my drawing . . . Do you know what it is?"

"It's a pair of girl's underpants!" shouted Marcel, one of the big boys.

"Does someone have a better idea?"

"It must be a map of Spain . . . "

This came from one of the older girls, Madeleine, who was very serious and had great presence of mind.

"Exactly, that's what it is. It's not a very good drawing, but it should help me to fill you in about what is happening in Spain. I think it's important for you to understand what is at stake in this war, because two days from now, we will be going into Paris to take part in a major demonstration in support of the Republic in Spain."

For most of us, a demonstration was above all an opportunity to get out of the orphanage, to go and shout and sing at the top of our lungs in the middle of a crowd; in short, it was a holiday, and whatever prompted it was secondary. And if it hadn't been for Arnold's solemn manner in gathering us all together, we would have allowed our joy to explode. But we could sense it would be inappropriate to hint at our futile reasons for wanting to take part in a demonstration. So we all looked sidelong at each other with a smile before focusing our interest on that map of Spain that looked nothing like a girl's underpants.

With the help of lines, arrows, pebbles and bits of wood, Arnold described the confrontation between the Republican and Nationalist troops in Spain. It was very interesting, but fairly complicated. There were other countries getting involved, Italy and Germany to be precise, on the side of the bad guys (the nationalists, led by Francisco Franco)—but nobody wanted to support the good guys (the Republicans, whom Franco had tried to overthrow by a military uprising). Still, there were people coming from all over, putting their lives at risk, to lend a hand to the Republicans. The way Arnold was talking about them, you could see right away that they were heroes, and that it wouldn't be long before he crossed the border and enrolled in the International Brigades, which were supported by the French Communist Party, among others.

At the end of this lesson about current events, Arnold suggested we make some banners and posters for the demonstration. He was so good at convincing us of the importance of the events on the other side of the border that we abandoned all thought of using our outing as an excuse to fool around. We worked for hours on end preparing our material, for we were professional demonstrators. No one could say that the children of L'Avenir Social—unlike France or England—had abandoned their Spanish friends!

The group that boarded a bus for Paris one fine spring morning was full of enthusiasm and passion. Roger Binet had the delicate task of carrying the banner which he and I had made, and we were very eager to display it the minute we reached Paris. After a long debate we had decided to write, "Solidarity with our Spanish Brothers." Roger would have liked to put something funnier, more tough-guy, or so he said, but I wanted to show on the contrary that even though we were children we understood the gravity of the situation. I took my participation in this political demonstration very seriously, and I had prepared for it with all my heart. In the end, it was really nice, all yellow, red, and purple, the colors of the Republican flag.

Twenty of us got off the bus at Buttes-Chaumont in Paris. From there we had to go to the Communards' Wall in the Père Lachaise Cemetery, where all the demonstrators were gathering. Arnold, Geneviève, an instructor by the name of Feller, and his wife Margot came with us. In the bus they had explained the rules of the game so we wouldn't get lost during the demonstration. Each adult had five or six children under his supervision. Each subgroup was divided in two, which meant teams of two or three children who had to keep an eye on each other. They allowed us to choose our teams, and I was with Roger, obviously, because we had to carry our banner together—our work of art! We thought we were very lucky, because the children under seven had not been allowed to come to the demonstration and we had only just turned seven.

We walked very quickly toward Père Lachaise—well, in

fact, because we were the youngest, we were trotting behind the others, and almost stumbled over our banner on more than one occasion. Other little groups were walking or running in the same direction as us with their signs, shouting and singing.

It was getting noisier and noisier, with chanting, and music, and horns blowing. People were screaming slogans through loudspeakers. All around I could see all sorts of signs and banners, not all of them referred to the war in Spain. I eventually understood that some of the crowd were demonstrating in support of the striking farm workers, another important cause in those days.

Arnold led us to a group of adults he seemed to know well who were shouting slogans for France to intervene on the side of the Republicans. Then we found our place. Roger and I unfurled our banner. We got jostled this way and that, and it wasn't easy to hold it above our heads, but in the end, two big kids who didn't have anything to carry helped us out. Once we had everything worked out, I added my voice to the general commotion. In our group there was a man with a big mustache who seemed to have a monopoly on the slogans. It was perfect, all you had to do was listen to him and you knew what to shout. I loved it.

"Solidarity among nations!" "*¡No pasarán!*" and the same slogan in French, "*Ils ne passeront pas!*"—they shall not pass. "Bread, peace and freedom for our Spanish friends!" The songs were tougher, because in the general uproar it was hard to make out the words, and Arnold had neglected this very important aspect of our preparation as demonstrators. We managed to join in with the others all the same, on certain refrains, only a few seconds behind them in what was a chaotic choir. I told myself I would ask them to put the revolutionary songs on the program of the choir at L'Avenir Social, which I had joined not long before.

Right in the middle of all the fun Arnold told us it was time to leave. Some of the kids thought the atmosphere at the demonstration was very exciting and they said his decision was too hasty: they called for a vote. Arnold put on his loud voice (but I am sure I saw a twinkle of amusement flash furtively in his eyes) and declared that this was a good idea, but that if we didn't want to miss the very last bus for the AS we would have to leave at once, unless we felt like walking all evening long and well into the night. His explanation won over the majority of the insurgents; only Marcel continued to shout, "Out of the question, democracy or death!" Geneviève went up to Arnold and murmured something in his ear. Arnold smiled and said, "Okay, those who want to leave now to catch the last bus, raise your hands." Everyone except Marcel raised their hand.

And thus our participation in the demonstration came to a very democratic end.

D uring my years at L'Avenir Social, there were a number of times when I went over the wall that separated us from the rest of the world. I knew we were not allowed to go out without permission. But if I thought it was for a good cause, and no one noticed my short absence, what possible harm could it do?

My first escapades were in the spring of 1938, under the reign of Feller, who replaced Henri at the head of L'Avenir Social for a few months. My relations with Henri had always been strained. I had never forgiven him for the extreme punishment I'd received at the beginning of my stay at the orphanage, and no doubt he had never forgiven me for my obvious hostility toward his son, Roland the owl. However, now when I think back on it, I tell myself that it wasn't simply a war of pride between us: in fact, our personalities were not compatible. Henri was a very serious sort, with very little sense of humor and a narrow, authoritarian vision of his role as director of L'Avenir Social. So I greatly appreciated the "Feller months," as we later called them among ourselves.

What I remember about Feller is that he was always badly dressed, his ginger hair was never combed, he had round blue eyes like marbles, and a good-humored communicative nature. I can still see him at his window calling to his wife, who was also his secretary, "Margot, come to the office!" to the tune of Schubert's *Unfinished Symphony*. (I learned the name of the work and of its composer thanks to Arnold, who was a great music lover and who always tried, generally to no avail, to transmit his passion to the children.)

One day Feller decided to hold a gardening contest to encourage a love of and respect for nature among the children. There were two gardens on the grounds of the orphanage: the kitchen garden, where Gros Pierre, the gardener, grew the vegetables that ended up in our plate, and another purely decorative garden. Gros Pierre was always pleased when the children showed an interest in his work, and he loved explaining how to choose the seeds, how to fertilize the plants and how to care for them when they were sick. He was delighted when Feller came up with this idea of a contest, where each participant would have a little plot that he or she could plant as they saw fit.

I was one of the first to sign up. I always loved watching Gros Pierre diligently sowing his seeds, and he would come back every day to see how they grew, and to encourage them. I knew that sometimes you had to pull the uglier plants out to give the others a chance to bloom, that you had to separate the babies from their mother and that you had to rethink the entire disposition of the garden on a regular basis, depending on the color, shape, and height of the plants. That was the part I liked best, when Gros Pierre would stand back and look at his garden then lean to one side and examine it from every angle, knitting his brows, chewing with great concentration on his right thumbnail. It was as if I could see the plants changing position in his head, like pieces on a chessboard.

Feller and Gros Pierre, with great pomp, called a meeting among all the children who had signed up for the L'Avenir Social in Bloom contest. There were a dozen of us who came, only four boys among them: Bernard, my first friend at the AS, whom I had found much less interesting once I was able to understand everything he said; Philippe, the intellectual of the group of older boys, not always popular, but whose sense of the ridiculous made me laugh; Marcel, the braggart; and me, Jules. The rest were girls, particularly the older ones I didn't know well at all, but there was also beautiful, shy Rolande, who was eight years old like me and had long brown curls: her presence sufficed to explain Marcel's participation in the contest.

"I'm very happy to see there are so many of you who are interested in the little contest that Pierre and I have devised. This will be a nice way for you to do something useful and have fun at the same time. You will acquire some notions of biology and natural sciences, and everyone at L'Avenir Social will be able to enjoy the beauty of our enhanced flower garden. Pierre, would you like to explain the rules of the contest to our young enthusiasts?"

Marcel was trying to make Rolande laugh by imitating Feller's big eyes and his excessive exuberance. At first Rolande blushed, then she gave him a very stern look, but Marcel seemed to interpret it as an invitation to continue.

"Marcel! This contest is open to everyone who wants to look after a garden. I must confess I have reason to doubt your motivation. Am I right?"

"Uh, no, I really like flowers."

"A garden takes a lot of work, my boy, you really have to want to do it."

"Well, yeah, I do want to do it."

 Some of the children giggled. Philippe rolled his eyes skyward. Gros Pierre tried to get back to more serious things.

"Feller, I could start by explaining the rules of the contest, and then the children will see if they want to take part, what do you think?"

"Yes, of course, go ahead."

"So, here we go. We will start by preparing a plot of land in the park near the pond, where everyone will have their own plot of roughly twelve square meters. Obviously, you will all help to prepare the terrain. In roughly three weeks, you'll be able to start sowing and planting. Before that, you'll have to come to me with your questions and read books about gardening. I have a few right here. I will provide the fertilizer, the soil, and the garden tools. I should have a few plants I can share at the beginning of spring and some bulbs and seeds I don't need, so there will be enough for everyone. Feller, do you have anything to add?"

"No. What about you, children, do you have any questions?"

"I was wondering if it would be possible to take normal plants . . . well, what I mean is, the wild plants that grow on the property here, or in the ditches along the roadside?" asked Rolande in her quiet voice.

"I don't see why not. What do you think, Feller?"

"On the grounds of the orphanage, that's fine. Plants from outside, that might be more difficult. But then, why not? Though I wouldn't like to see you heading off with a huge shovel every time we leave the grounds on an excursion. Is that clear?"

We nodded. Feller called an end to the meeting, and the gong for dinner went just then, so we got up without saying thank you or goodbye, and rushed to the refectory. I already had a few ideas for my garden. During dinner, Marcel regaled us with an imitation of Gros Pierre. He adopted his most sententious air and came out with his finest rolled *r*'s: "We are going to plant the garrrden, with the earrrth and the tools. It is verrry difficult. You'll have to rrrread books. Marrrcel, do you think you can?" He was a real idiot, that Marcel, but he did have a gift for imitating people.

My mother was due to visit two days later, so I decided I would order my seeds through her; as she always came to the orphanage by bus, I couldn't ask her to bring anything too cumbersome. I'd already begun leafing through Gros Pierre's gardening books. I was very excited about the contest, and after that first official meeting I began looking closely at all the gardens on the way to school, obliging myself to form an opinion about each one: "I like this one," or "That one is pretty but a bit too tidy," or even "That is exactly what I do *not* want to do." Since all the children at L'Avenir Social went to the same school, all I could use these gardens for was inspiration, without copying anything, because that would be too obvious and diminish my chances of winning.

For the first time since I had come to L'Avenir Social, I was looking forward to my mother's visit. I had made up a list of the seeds I wanted her to get for me, in decreasing order of importance: "Poppies, pansies, zinnias, campanula, asters, and cosmos," to which I added yellow or orange dahlia bulbs. I wanted a country garden, with bright colors.

My mother's visit went fairly well this time; I was the one who did nearly all the talking. I showed her the garden, and explained the rules of the contest. I don't know how much she understood, but thanks to my list, where everything was clearly indicated, she couldn't go wrong. The only time I got a little bit annoyed was when I asked her to come back within four weeks and I could tell from her somewhat vague reaction that she wasn't taking my request very seriously. Her usual "*Oui, oui*" really annoyed me, and I insisted and explained that otherwise she might as well not come at all, because it would be too late for the contest. She promised she'd be there "as soon as possible." The way she put it was not precise enough to my liking, but there was nothing more I could do, other than to hope she would prove to me that I could count on her, in spite of all the lies she had told me when I was little.

So I was immensely relieved when roughly five weeks after this meeting, Arnold informed me that Lena would be coming the very next day. I had begun to think that she had forgotten all about me . . . but she hadn't, and I felt bad about not trusting her.

"Hello, my little Julek."

"Hello, Lena. How are you?"

"Fine, fine, and you?"

I resigned myself to joking about this and that with her; I would wait a while before referring to the matter that truly interested me. After a while she was the one who brought it up.

"I have this thing for you. You want?"

"Yes, of course!"

Lena took a little paper package from her big canvas bag. She handed it to me. I took it. And opened it. Little chocolate sweets . . .

"But you have my seeds, too, don't you?"

"*Oui, oui*," she said, somewhat surprised by my reaction.

"So where are they?"

She just stared at me.

"The seeds, remember, I gave you a list, flowers, the names of flowers on a piece of paper?"

"Ah, *oui, oui*, flowers! But I have chocolates. Flowers, after. Next time."

I felt my ears go warm. I wanted to stand up, and take her by the shoulders, and shake her very hard. But I went on sitting there, not saying a thing, waiting for something to make this woman disappear from my sight. Since she didn't know what else to say, Lena soon decided that it was time for her to leave. She gave me a kiss—how annoying—and smiled at me—how annoying—and gave me a hug—all right, is that it now?—and turned around and left.

I was furious. I went out into the park and ran to hide in my secret refuge. On my way I gave a kick to a huge rock. Ouch! The pain had a calming effect on my mind. I curled up in a ball and spent a long time mulling over all the reasons I had to be angry with Lena, and there were plenty of them. "I can never trust her. You can't count on her, she doesn't do anything I ask her to do, but she always says, '*Oui, oui*,' because she doesn't even have the balls to say, 'You know, I don't give a damn about your garden thing,' which is the truth, because she doesn't give a damn about anything concerning me. Well, she won't get away with it, just because she's too stupid to remember a little teeny tiny favor doesn't mean I can't still have the most beautiful garden in the contest." I had to find a solution, and fast, because the planting period had already begun.

And suddenly the solution came to me, in all its splendor, its logic, and its simplicity.

The very next morning, straight after breakfast, I went down to the bottom of the garden, behind the pond, where the tall shrubbery concealed a stone wall. Clinging with all my strength with my little fingers to the few protruding stones, I hoisted myself to the top of the wall. Without even looking behind me, I jumped down to the other side, landing on an uncultivated plot of land between two houses with their gardens nicely arranged. No need to look any further on my first sortie. I headed to the right, keeping my eyes on the little white house half hidden by tall trees. This was perfect. I blended in with the shade of the trees, and no one could see me.

It became trickier when I got to the garden, which was located right out in the sunlight. I observed it from a distance, and gave some thought to what might interest me. As I hadn't taken any tools, I would have to choose something I could dig up with my hands. Then I thought, I know, I've got it: irises. I recognized their long flat leaves in a shadier part of the garden. I glanced once again at the house, took a deep breath and rushed forward, practically crawling, as if I were about to ambush someone. First of all I tried to dig up some big iris plants, but the soil where they were planted was hard and compact, and I couldn't get my fingers under the bulbs. I looked all around: in an airier corner of the garden that seemed to have been recently planted, I saw some little irises with very pale leaves, and crept toward them. This time, it worked! I dug up three or four at first and was getting ready to leave, then changed my mind, reasoning that it would be better to make the best use of the risk I was taking. I chose four more, which didn't go with the rest of that garden anyway . . . and while I was at it, why not an additional three, and I buried them deep in my pockets.

Just as I was about to head back, I heard a door slam. Darn! I tried to disappear behind a little bush. I could hear a little girl talking. She seemed to be having a long conversation . . . The voice was coming closer, and before long I could make out what she was saying. "And if you disobey me one more time, you will stay in a drawer all summer long. Do you understand, Mathilde? In the meantime, I am taking you out to the garden to be punished." I could hear the stifled sound of an object falling into the grass. "I'll come back later to see if you have calmed down." I waited a little bit longer. The door slammed again. I got up quietly, and stole slowly into the shade of the trees, and then I made a dash to the wall, climbed over, and soon I was back home at L'Avenir Social, and no one the wiser!

The next day I went through the same rigmarole again, and the day after that. Each time, I "visited" a different garden to make sure I would have a nice variety of flowers. I was getting better organized. I took a little bag with me, and a little garden shovel, with which I could dig up some of the more delicate plants. On my fourth expedition, I was on my way back to the orphanage, being very careful not to damage the pretty anemone plants at the bottom of my bag, and when I reached the spot where I had to climb over the wall, I looked up, and there at the top, watching me, arms crossed and a half smile on his face, was Arnold.

"Good harvest?"

I was speechless.

"Come on, show me what you have hidden in your bag."

I obeyed.

"Those are nice plants you have there. I don't know much about them, can you tell me what they are?"

"Uh . . . anemones."

"And they'll grow into pretty flowers?"

"Uh-huh."

"Well, wouldn't you know, I've had some complaints from people in the neighborhood saying that one of our children has been raiding their borders. They're none too pleased, as you can imagine, right? Well, we won't make a huge thing about it. I want you to swear that you will never get up to these shenanigans again, that you will never steal any plants or anything else from the orphanage's neighbors."

"I swear."

"Perfect. Now go and plant your little leaves whose name I've forgotten, and we won't mention it again."

In this whole garden contest business, the thing that made the strongest impression on me, besides Arnold's surprising leniency, was the fact that I didn't win the contest, in spite of the originality of my little garden. I didn't even get second prize. I can't remember who won, but I thought it was very unfair that I was not one of the finalists. It was only years later that I understood that I had been disqualified for having resorted to an illegal procedure.

I recovered quickly enough from my disappointment, and a year later I was the only contest participant who was still tending his little garden. Maybe it had something to do with my thieving from the neighbors' yards; maybe I felt some sort of responsibility toward my plants, because I wanted to give them as good a life as they would have had if I had never kidnapped them.

CHAPTER 12
The Grand Duke

Ever since our vacation on the Île de Ré, I had been dreaming of becoming an animal trainer. Now I had found a new vocation: veterinarian. This was even better, because it would mean truly helping animals, instead of using them for the amusement of humans. This was driven home to me one day when I found a wounded creature on the grounds of L'Avenir Social. And it was no ordinary creature, like a squirrel, or a tit . . . It was an owl. When I found him, he was hiding in the bushes. There was something wrong with his wing, and he held it stiffly alongside his body. There was no blood, just a little patch on the wing where some feathers were missing.

I looked after my little owl—baptized the Grand Duke—for nearly ten days. In the beginning, I acted the hunter: I found worms for him, and frogs; I even brought him a dead mouse which one of the neighborhood cats had left almost intact. After a while I opted for a simpler solution: scraps of raw meat from the kitchen, obtained thanks to my imploring gaze as an adoptive father. As soon as he was better, I would let him venture out of the cage from time to time. Gros Pierre agreed to lend me his toolshed for a first trial run at setting him free. Roger was chosen as my partner for the operation.

Roger and I were walking home from school, and I would have liked to discuss the matter with him, but I was afraid of prying ears. I didn't want the Grand Duke's stroll to turn into a show.

"It would be better if we keep the lights off while we watch the aristocracy go by."

Roger didn't say anything.

"Don't you think?"

I was trying to speak code language to Roger, but visibly it wasn't working. The fact is, we had just had an exam about the French Revolution at school, and Roger was not very pleased with his answers. My subtle message must have his anxiety at being a very mediocre pupil flooding back.

When we got back to the orphanage, we rushed to see the Grand Duke, who was asleep in his cage. I spoke to him quietly. He moved a bit, but he still seemed drowsy. That didn't matter, Roger and I lifted the cage and carried it into the toolshed.

"We're going to open your cage, your Royal Highness, but it's just so that you can take a little walk, and after that you'll go back in for the night. If everything goes well, we'll try it again."

He was listening attentively. He seemed to approve of the plan. I was still hesitating. Roger looked at me, impatiently. Okay, all right . . . I opened the cage.

Nothing happened. The Grand Duke did not seem to grasp the new possibilities open to him. After a few moments, Roger and I looked at each other, disappointed.

"What should we do? Maybe we should shake him up a bit."

"Yeah, for sure we can't stay here like idiots until dinnertime waiting for some owl to understand that the door to his cage is open."

"I should have brought something to eat . . . "

"Maybe he likes it in there so much he's afraid to come out."

"Keep a close eye on him, I'll be back."

I upended every pebble on the path looking for worms. I

had just found a sticky little insect when I heard shouts from the toolshed. I rushed over. I tried to open the door, but it was stuck.

"Careful, he mustn't get out," called Roger. "I'm going to crack the door open a bit and you come in very quickly, all right?"

"Yes, yes . . . Come on, hurry up!"

Inside, it took a few seconds for my eyes to adjust to the darkness. I could see the cage was open, and empty . . .

"He's up there, just under the roof!"

"Did he fly?"

"Well, yeah, he didn't climb up there like a mountaineer."

"But then that means that he's all better! Your Royal Highness, you're all better, that's wonderful! You can fly again."

My protégé seemed to be greatly enjoying walking along the shelves in the toolshed. Roger and I stayed there watching him in silence. The dinner gong brought us back to reality.

"Darn! We have to get him back in his cage!"

"I found a worm just now, maybe that will attract him."

"What are you doing, boys, it's dinnertime!"

It was Gros Pierre.

"We can't get the owl back in his cage!"

Then it all happened very quickly. Gros Pierre opened the door, I hurried to close it, I stumbled over a box full of tools, Roger gave a shout, I heard things falling over, a rustling of wings, and I saw a shadow fly through the door of the shed. I stood up like a flash and reached out my arms in hopes of catching the bird. No such luck. The shadow flew away toward the trees on the far side of the orphanage's stone wall.

"Grand Duke, come back, please!"

Too late. He was already gone.

"Are you coming to eat, Jules?"

How could I have any appetite! Sometimes Roger is truly insensitive, he really deserves his nickname Robinet the water faucet. I asked him not to tell anyone what had just happened, I was sure that some of the kids would be only too pleased to hear about our misadventure. Like Roland, who looked like an owl, so he didn't like competition . . .

It took me a long time to fall asleep that night. I kept thinking about what had happened, and wondered what I could have done to prevent my protégé from escaping; I told myself it would not have taken much for things to turn out differently, and I wouldn't have this big lump in my throat. The Grand Duke had begun to matter a lot in my life.

The next morning, Gros Pierre came to see me straight after breakfast.

"Hey there, Julot, how are you? Ah, you're looking a bit bleary-eyed. I might have some good news for you. There were people in the village this morning talking about some owl hooting all night long and keeping them awake. I thought it might be the Grand Duke, perhaps he was sad not to be here anymore. I wouldn't be surprised if he came back."

"And where do they live, those people who didn't sleep all night?"

"Near the Dumoutiers' farm."

"Yeah, that's not that close . . . "

"For the Grand Duke it's nothing, just a few flaps of his wings and he'll be here."

Well, if the Grand Duke wasn't that far away, then I had an idea that might work. I absolutely had to talk it over with Roger.

"The problem is how to catch him. He won't let just anybody do it. You're the one who has to do it . . . " said Roger.

"Yeah, but what if he doesn't want to go back in his cage?"

"I think he misses you."

"I don't know . . . "

"You know what? We'll climb over the wall tonight and go looking for him."

It didn't take much for Roger to convince me.

An hour after bedtime, Roger and I tiptoed out of the dormitory. It was a magnificent night, the moon was almost full, casting the brilliant light we needed for our mission. We went to the spot where the wall was a little lower. Roger gave me a leg up, and I helped to tug him up after me.

For a while we walked without speaking, like two hunters on the lookout. Roger was the one who broke the silence.

"What do we do if we find him?"

"Well, that will depend if he's high up in a tree or within reach. There are too many factors to be taken into consideration, we'll see when the time comes."

Roger did not seem the least bit convinced by my answer, and I got the impression that the cold air was getting the better of his faith in our undertaking. But because he was a good sort, he strode on with determination, looking all around him like a warrior in enemy terrain.

The night was very calm. From time to time a gust of wind rustled a few leaves along the pavement, a dog barked as we went by, or some shutters banged at their window . . .

When we reached the woods, we skirted them to the path that led into them. Still no sign of my bird. I suggested we split up, and I headed toward the river while Roger went into the heart of the woods. Perhaps if the Grand Duke saw me on my own he would rush up to me. But the ambient silence did not leave me much hope. Roughly an hour later, we met up again. Roger was discouraged.

"He obviously isn't in these woods. I'm willing to look some more, but we have no idea which way to go."

"Follow me. We can't give up yet, I sense that he's not far away."

"If you say so . . . "

And off we went again. There was even a certain thrill about walking around in the middle of the night and visiting the hidden recesses of Villette-aux-Aulnes. We went down muddy paths into forbidden fields, and saw a baby hare that seemed to have lost its mother. And when dawn broke, we were on the road leading from Villette-aux-Aulnes to Mitry-Mory, a good hour away from the orphanage.

"I'm hungry. We should try and get back in time for breakfast, don't you think?"

I nodded. I had to face the facts: The Grand Duke was nowhere to be found.

"You looked after him so well that he doesn't need you anymore. You should become a veterinarian later, you have a real vocation."

Roger can be really kind.

A pink light appeared behind the blue clouds at the end of the road. The world was beginning to wake up, we could hear the sounds of animals in the farms, roosters proclaiming the arrival of the new day, and the engine of the first car heading down the road. We were nearly there when we heard shouting. Darn! The children were out looking for us, we had arrived too late for our absence to go unnoticed.

"We can't climb over the wall now, we'll be in for a terrible thrashing."

"I'm so hungry!"

"If we go back now, they're not going to welcome us with open arms or offer us anything to eat. Let's try and find something in the neighbors' fields or gardens."

We turned our back on the orphanage and headed off again.

B y nightfall we couldn't take it anymore: we had hardly eaten a thing all day, and that night was looking to be colder than the previous one. I was so hungry I couldn't even think straight or come up with a plan. So I followed Roger docilely and agreed to all his suggestions.

"When everyone is in bed, we go over the wall and we run and hide in the toilets at the end of the yard. Afterwards, when everyone's asleep, we'll sneak into our beds."

"All right."

I don't know whether we really believed that the strategy would enable us to return without suffering any consequences. We were two eight-year-old boys who had been missing for over twelve hours. Maybe we were being driven by some sort of magical thinking, like an ostrich that believes he's hidden when he puts his head in the sand, and we imagined that the next day our lives would pick up where they had left off before our escapade.

Our mission "Return to L'Avenir Social" failed because we were just too tired and hungry. We couldn't wait the time we should, and we went to hide in the toilets before nightfall.

After a few minutes, there was a loud muted sound at the door.

"Come on, out of there, right now!"

Hoping for some sudden reversal of the situation, Roger and I stopped breathing, moving, or even thinking.

"Roger and Jules, I know you're in there, don't be stupid,

come out at once! If you force me to break the door down it won't make things any better for you!"

I recognized the voice of Georges, one of the instructors. No two ways about it: we were trapped like mice! Roger was the one who gave the signal to surrender, by clearing his throat. I opened the door to the shed, and we both walked out, heads down, waiting, resigned, for whatever came next.

"Follow me!"

Georges grabbed us by the arm and shoved us, or pulled us, I'm not sure which, toward the orphanage and then up to our dear director's office. He knocked on the door. From the other side came a resounding and not very inviting "Come in." But maybe it just sounded that way to me because I was so aware of how precarious a situation we were in.

"Aha! So you found our two little runaways! Where were they hiding?"

"I saw them come over the wall and hide in the toilets at the end of the yard."

"So, you went for a little stroll, and when you had had enough, you simply returned to the fold. I hope you weren't expecting a warm welcome! The police are out looking for you! Don't you think they have other fish to fry? Georges, would you please go and inform the police that our two good-for-nothings have come back?"

"I'm on my way."

"Do you have anything to say in your defense? Would you like to explain what was going on in your little heads, or at least try?"

We were both speechless.

"Very convincing . . . "

I focused all my attention on the director's scarlet cheeks. I knew their color was not a good sign, that he was surely in the mood to give us a spectacular thrashing. But I was wrong, because he was in the process of fomenting a far more diabolical plan, one which would make me regret the thrashing I did not receive.

"Stay here, I'll be back."

He locked the door behind him as he went out.

"Couldn't he give us something to eat first and yell at us afterwards?" moaned Roger.

It was pointless to reply, even though I agreed with him. Any punishment would seem welcome after several mouthfuls of a good hot meal.

After what seemed like ages, Henri returned. "You two, come with me!"

We followed him down the corridor. We were not very surprised to see we were not going in the direction of the refectory. Henri led us out into the courtyard, where all the children in the orphanage were lined up in rows. Not saying a word, he shoved us into the center of the courtyard and left us alone, facing the children. What were we supposed to do? Apologize to the others for having obliged them to spend the day looking for us? Maybe if we apologized there and then, we could move onto something else. I lifted my head a little and my gaze fell upon Bernard, the first in the row. When his eyes met mine, he looked down. He seemed unhappy, or ill at ease. This was not a good sign, I could tell.

"Go ahead, Bernard, we'll start with you."

That was Henri speaking. What would start with Bernard?

Bernard walked over to Roger to start with, still looking at the ground. Suddenly, quite unexpectedly, he slapped him a few times on the back, then very quickly came over to me, gave me something vaguely resembling a punch—except it didn't hurt at all—then ran back to the other children.

"Next!" shouted the director.

Then it was Daniel's turn. He was one of the littlest kids; he advanced forward and went through the same rigmarole.

I don't know how long that strange session of public punishment lasted, perhaps an hour, perhaps far less, but there are two things I know for sure: most of the children did not want to hurt us—except for Roland and two or three other boys who got carried away—and the physical pain was nowhere near as unpleasant as the burning feeling deep in my chest which I would only be able to put a name to much later: humiliation.

I would never forgive Henri for that cruel punishment, which contravened all the progressive rules regarding education that were in force at L'Avenir Social. Would Geneviève and Arnold, who were away on vacation when it happened, have been able to curb Henri's zeal? Most of the instructors at L'Avenir Social must have been at odds with our director's pedagogical vision . . . and most of the children, too.

When all is said and done, this adventure had a positive effect on my life. For a start, as I'll explain, it sealed my friendship with Geneviève—a friendship that would last until well after the war and my departure from Europe. And it would reinforce my pleasure in reading. Because Henri did not stop there. After all the children had beaten us, we were deprived of any verbal contact with them. No one was allowed to speak to us until we had asked forgiveness for our misbehavior and promised never to do it again. Roger quickly accepted the director's conditions; I did not hold it against him, everyone has their own values. But for me it was out of the question to ask anyone for forgiveness: no one had been willing to listen to our story, and in my opinion it did not warrant such a punishment, so I was prepared to wall myself up in silence until the end of time. Our escapade had shown me that I was not a good candidate for hunger strikes, but I was pleased to discover that I had a certain talent for resistance.

Since no one was allowed to speak or play with me, I spent all my free time reading. My resistance lasted the length of two and a half novels: *Tarzan of the Apes*, which I was reading for the third time; Jack London's *White Fang*; and half of *The Jungle Book*. It was Geneviève who called an end to my mutiny. To do so, she got out the big guns: candy.

I was sitting in the visitors' drawing room pretending to read—in fact I was listening to the shouts of the children, who had organized an acrobatics contest—when Geneviève came in and sat down next to me.

"Jules, I have something for you in my room. Will you come with me?"

"Uh, I guess so."

I went with Geneviève up to the third floor. This was the first time I had ever seen one of the instructors' rooms. Geneviève's was small, with almost no decoration, but it was full of books and magazines: on the shelves, on the night table, on a tiny desk, on the floor . . . Geneviève sat down on the bed and motioned to me to take the chair next to the desk. She smiled and said, "If you like, I can lend you some books. Would you like that?"

"Yes. I think that before long I'll have read everything interesting in the orphanage library. And at school I'm not allowed to borrow the books for grown-ups."

"At your age, I didn't like children's books either. But I shall still have to advise you, because some of them won't be interesting for a boy your age, even as sharp as you are . . . Here, I have a big bag of full of candy, there's too much for me, if you want some, help yourself."

Too much candy! What an idea! I knew you shouldn't allow yourself to be bought by the enemy, but since Geneviève had always behaved kindly toward me, it was hard to remain defiant around her. I could have a piece or two of candy . . . no one would be the wiser.

"You know, I'm impressed to see how well you have kept to the line of conduct you set for yourself, even though it can't be much fun not to play or speak with the other children any-more."

Something inside me whispered a warning to be careful when answering.

"When you have convictions," I said, "you have to be con-sistent. I think I shouldn't have to apologize for wanting to find my owl; I looked after him for a long time and perhaps he wasn't ready to be set free again."

"Of course . . . but you could have gone about it differently. If you had talked about it with an instructor, we could have put together a search party with all the children from L'Avenir Social. It might even have been more efficient."

This had never occurred to me.

"If every time one of the children thought they had a good reason to go outside L'Avenir Social they climbed over the wall, can you imagine what it would be like for us? I am sure Henri was very worried. He must have been afraid he might never find you again."

"But he really overreacted, all the same. It was horrible to be beaten by all the children, it was like being in a Roman arena. And he really enjoyed watching the kids hit us. I'll never forgive him."

"I understand that it must have been painful, humiliating, I understand . . . "

Geneviève broke off; she seemed to be hunting for her words.

"I'm not saying I agree with what he did. If Arnold and I had been there, we would have been against it, believe me, this session of . . . But we can't have the children jumping over the wall in secret. If you promise me never to run away again, I think I'll be able to convince Henri to put an end to your pun-ishment."

We talked a little bit more, about my punishment and a few other things, and in the end, after I had eaten some more candy, I had to admit that Geneviève was right. And I promised not to climb over the wall. A promise I would keep from that day on . . . Well, almost, except for one time when out of solidarity I went with the big kids who refused to get their heads shaven when it was the only remedy for the lice epidemic raging at L'Avenir Social. But I won't go into that story, because it is time to get back to more serious things: politics.

After our participation in the demonstration in support of the Republicans in Spain, the political fervor of a number of children at L'Avenir Social increased. Naturally I belonged to this politicized elite. We often talked with Arnold about the evolution of the situation in Spain. Unfortunately, the news was always bad.

Arnold didn't only talk about Spain, he also taught us about the situation elsewhere in the world. We were proud to be considered old enough to understand what was at stake in the modern world. We were proud to be on the right side, that of communism, and we intended to do whatever it took, as long as we had to, to get France to join the Communist International alongside the USSR.

One day we were told a great event was in store, the very next day: a visit from some Soviet dignitaries. Roger and I were enchanted: real flesh and blood Soviet Communists in our orphanage! Philippe too was thrilled with the news. For the rest of the day, we saw him walking around with a book in his hand, even outdoors; while everyone else was playing, he had his nose buried in his book. It was as if he were studying to take an exam to enter the Supreme Soviet (I didn't know exactly what that was, but I thought the term "Supreme Soviet" was full of grandeur and nobility, however contradictory that might seem).

The next day I got up earlier than usual and I left the dormitory without a sound, because I wanted to be sure not to miss the arrival of the Soviets. I came upon Philippe, who was sitting on a bench near the front door, still completely absorbed by his reading. The orphanage was silent; clearly the dignitaries would not be arriving anytime soon. I sat down next to Philippe, curious to find out what sort of book could be hypnotizing him to such a degree.

"What do you want, Jules?"

"I haven't seen you once without that book in your hand since yesterday. I just wanted to know what it was."

"I'd be surprised if it interested you."

"Well, I am interested, since I asked you."

"No, what I mean is . . . Anyway, suit yourself. The book is *The Communist Manifesto.* I want to be well prepared, I want to show that even children can have an enlightened vision of politics."

"And is it interesting to read? Could you lend it to me?"

"'But not only has the bourgeoisie forged the weapons that bring death to itself; it has also called into existence the men who are to wield those weapons—the modern working class— the proletarians.

"'In proportion as the bourgeoisie, i.e. capital, is developed, in the same proportion is the proletariat, the modern working class, developed—a class of laborers, who live only so long as they find work, and who find work only so long as their labour increases capital. These labourers, who must sell themselves piecemeal, are a commodity, like every other article of commerce . . . '"

I didn't dare show him that I was all at sea. As I had, regardless, a solid political background—I knew, for example, that the bourgeois were on one side and the proletariat on the other, and that we communists believed in the might of the proletariat—but I didn't expect to feel so stupid upon hearing this famous manifesto . . . I wanted to ask Philippe to explain it to me somewhat, so that I would be ready, too, to meet the

Soviets, but to do that I would have to admit I hadn't under-stood a thing, and something inside wouldn't let me do that.

"So, my Julot, what do you think?"

"Yeah, well, there's nothing very new in it, however . . . "

"Maybe not, but I think it shows very clearly why we are bound to win and why the bourgeoisie is doomed to perish."

"Indeed, it does show that . . . "

While we were talking, the orphanage gradually began to stir. First we could hear the sounds of dishes clattering in the refectory, and then a crescendo of children's voices: they were clearly very excited by the thought of the great day we were about to experience. Philippe paid no more attention to me and went back to his reading.

At breakfast Albert came in and whispered something in the director's ear. Henri took his handkerchief, quickly wiped the corners of his mouth (I was always impressed to see how he con-centrated when performing this useless act, given that he was hardly the type to make a mess while eating), whispered some-thing in Arnold's ear in return, then stood up and left the refec-tory. Arnold swallowed his coffee in one gulp and got up in turn.

"Arnold, have the Soviet comrades arrived?"

"Yes, Jules, I'm going to meet them. Since I speak some Russian, Henri wants me to be with him during the visit."

"Are we going to be able to talk to them?" asked Philippe, his cheeks flushed and his eyes shining.

I started laughing hysterically to see Philippe looking so colorful.

"Hey, why are you laughing like that, you idiot?"

"Whoa, calm down! I have to get there right away, but I promise to pass on your request to Henri. Would anyone else like to talk with them?"

Five or six children raised their hands, including Roger and me, of course.

"I'm glad that you're so interested. I can't guarantee anything, I don't know how long they intend to stay, but I'll see what I can do."

After Arnold left, everyone got even more excited. We were all speaking at the same time, and throwing things across the refectory at each other.

"Hey, Robinet, do you think the Soviets have water faucets?"

"I bet you can't even find the Soviet Union on a map. If you had to lead us there for a meeting with the comrades, we'd all die of shame before getting close!"

"Did you see what a bright red color Philippe's ears were? It was to impress the Communists!"

Philippe didn't answer, he just took on his air of an adult who is disappointed by a child's puerile behavior, and got up to take his plate to the basin full of dirty dishes. I decided to follow him; I didn't feel like goofing off with the others and giving L'Avenir Social a bad image.

After leaving the refectory Philippe headed toward the director's office. I acted as if it was perfectly natural for me to trail along behind him. The door to the director's office was closed, and we couldn't hear any voices. Philippe and I looked at each other, hesitating. "Maybe they're outside?" I said very quietly, in hopes I'd be forgiven for my incongruous hysterical laughter earlier. Philippe didn't answer, but headed toward the door leading to the garden. We went outside. Henri and Arnold were there, with four strange men, and they were showing them Gros Pierre's garden (and my little plot at the same time). These gentlemen were . . . how to put it . . . very disappointing. Maybe I was naïve, but I thought they would be wearing their shirts open at the collar, like the revolutionaries in Russian films. No, they were wearing suits and ties. And while Arnold was waving his arms, showing them things left and right, all they did was nod their heads from time to time, halfheartedly.

Philippe and I, and then Roger and his brother Pierre, who came to join us, followed them around during their entire visit, to be sure to be the first to speak to them if the opportunity arose. The opportunity never arose and, in fact, it was better that way, because we no longer felt like talking to these individuals who looked like civil servants, like bureaucrats, with their gray complexion and their dull eyes.

That night, while he was next to me washing his face, Roger said, "What did you think of them, then, the Soviets?"

"Well, I'd imagined them differently."

"Me too . . . maybe those were the only ones who were available, maybe the other ones, the real ones, were too busy doing more important things for the Revolution than visiting an orphanage in a little village in the middle of nowhere. Maybe it's just because they couldn't understand Arnold's Russian that they looked so miserable."

"Maybe . . . "

Roger was making a desperate effort to keep that handful of men in ties from ruining the fine image he had of our Soviet brothers. For the time being I was too disappointed to try to rescue anything with my imagination. Maybe they sent us the dullest ones because the others, the real ones, didn't have time. But who was to say they weren't all like that? I fell asleep very quickly, I didn't want to have to think anymore about the day gone by.

T he grown-ups were talking more and more of war. According to some, war was inevitable. I tried to grill Arnold about it, but contrary to his usual manner, he was very vague with his replies. I understood that we were against Germany and Italy, the two countries supporting Franco in Spain. But who would attack who, and why? These questions remained unanswered. Arnold adopted his "it's not for children" air as soon as I tried to scratch the surface, and this surprised me because, frankly, it wasn't like him. I remained unruffled and decided to ask Geneviève, whom I suspected—even though she rarely talked politics with us—of knowing at least as much about the question as Arnold did. One day when I was returning a book she had lent me, I asked if I could stay in her room—something I hadn't done since her candy victory—to discuss something important.

"Of course you can, my little Julot."

"Good. You have to explain this business about imminent war with the Germans and the Italians, well, against them, I mean."

I tried to imply that I already knew quite a bit, so no need to handle me with kid gloves.

"Is that all you want?"

"Yes, that's all."

"You know, it's never that simple, a matter like this. First, you have to know what a dictator is."

"I know what a dictator is, they're like Hitler and Mussolini, they're people who do whatever they want, who think they're the king and they don't care about the will of their people."

"In a way, yes. Listen, I'll do my best, but it's complicated."

"Take your time, I'm not in a hurry."

"Okay, fine. In fact, the reason everybody thinks that war is imminent is because Hitler keeps on threatening different countries. Every time it's for a new reason—he claims, for example, than such and such a territory should belong to Germany, and if they don't give it to him, he's going to go to war. He's already annexed Austria, and now he wants to do the same thing with Czechoslovakia, or with part of the country anyway. Do you follow?"

"And does he want to annex France, too?"

"He hasn't said so for the time being, but there are parts of France that used to belong to Germany, so, obviously . . . In any case, we can't just let him do what he wants in Europe without stepping in."

I was glad that Geneviève had agreed to try and explain it all to me, but I still wasn't satisfied. Fair enough, we couldn't let Hitler do as he pleased, but was that really sufficient reason to go to war, when children might die? On the newsreels at the movies I had seen pictures of the bombing in a little village in Spain. You could see a whole lot of dead children.

When we went back to school in the fall, this war business continued to worry me. Even Liliane, our teacher, who was not particularly clued in on politics, decided she had to talk to us about it. We even had an entire class about the Great War. You couldn't say it was exactly reassuring. I made some skillful calculations: I was almost nine years old, and if a world war generally lasted four years, I would be roughly thirteen when the next one was over. So I had to survive to the age of thirteen, and after that things should be okay. This became my main goal in life.

All week long, when we walked home from school, war was

the only topic of conversation. Because of the images of Spain on the newsreels, we all knew that children were the first ones who were attacked when there was a war. So an orphanage, you can imagine! It became clear that we needed a plan to save our skins, we had to react very quickly if war broke out, because the orphanage could be bombed on the very first day.

Should we hide in the cellar? Or run away? It was an easy decision: most of the children thought we should run away. But should we run away all together? Or in little groups? Or each of us on our own? And where should we go? Into the forest? Should we hide in the countryside, under the haystacks? Seek refuge with the farmers?

Together with Roger and his brother we came up with an escape plan. Like me, Roger and Pierre were not actual orphans: they had a father who lived not far from Paris. Given the fact that he was an alcoholic, we figured the Germans would have no reason to fear him or to attack him, so we could go and hide with him. They hadn't had any news from him for a while, so for the first stage in elaborating our escape plan Pierre was charged with finding out where he lived. Then we would have to find out the various ways to get there, because some of the roads might be cut off or impassable because of the bombings. We had already packed some nonperishable food in Pierre's rucksack. Of the three of us he was the only one who had a rucksack. My job was to find two more.

One day at the end of September, in the midst of this tense atmosphere, a small group of children from the orphanage, myself included, took the bus to go to Paris to see *Snow White and the Seven Dwarfs*.

When we got to Paris the bus had to take a detour—its normal route was blocked off because of a massive demonstration. It was as if everyone in Paris was out in the street. Accompanying us on the outing were Geneviève and Simone, an instructor who had arrived at L'Avenir Social not long before. They seemed surprised to see so many people in the street. As the bus hadn't moved for quite a while, Geneviève asked the driver to let her out, so she could go and find out what was going on. After a few minutes she came back.

"Children, I don't think we're going to make it to the movie in time. I suggest we get out of this bus and try to catch another that will take us back to the orphanage."

"But what is the demonstration for?"

"A peace treaty has been signed with Germany."

We greeted the good news with shouts of joy. We could forget our plans to run away, no need to leave L'Avenir Social, no need to go looking for Old Man Binet! The joyful atmosphere that reigned in the streets of Paris infected us, and as we left the bus we raised our voices in unison with the other demonstrators. I noticed that Geneviève did not seem as carried away as we did, but I was too happy to dwell on the fact or try to find out why she was so halfhearted.

In the days that followed the peace treaty, the atmosphere at the orphanage was euphoric and relaxed. We were able to admit how frightened we had been by what had seemed an inevitable war, how vulnerable we had felt as orphans or abandoned children, and how happy we were now to be able to go on living at L'Avenir Social with the people who were our true family.

There was something bothering me, however. The adults didn't seem to share our joy. To be clear in my own mind about it, I went to see Arnold.

"You are right, my Julot, we're not too pleased with this peace treaty, or at least I don't think it was the right decision. If the agreement was signed, once again it is because we've yielded to Hitler's demands, and we've allowed him to annex certain territories in exchange for a promise of peace. But how far will it go? Are we going to allow him to nibble away at

Europe in order to avoid a war which, in my opinion, will break out anyway if Hitler remains in power in Germany? How can we believe this madman's promises?"

I didn't know what to say. I was so disappointed by what Arnold had just told me that I was sorry I had even asked. All my joy and relief vanished.

"Don't make such a face, Julot. Maybe I'm wrong, you know, most people don't share my opinion."

"Maybe not, but you know more about politics than most people."

I didn't feel like prolonging the discussion. I told Arnold that I had homework to finish and I went to find refuge at the very top of a tree at the end of the yard. I needed to think about it all. I didn't know whether I ought to share the bad news with the Binet brothers or whether it would be better to spare them. Pierre had been so happy at the thought he wouldn't have to go and live with his father.

S pring, 1939. Things were not getting better. There were nights I could not sleep from thinking about the war. Now everyone believed it was imminent. And I had no one left to talk to about the events, because Geneviève and Arnold had left L'Avenir Social. One day they simply came to say goodbye. I was so upset, so sad, that I didn't even ask them why they were leaving. Both of them were very upset.

A gloom settled over the orphanage. We didn't eat as well as we used to, we were told they had to save money, make sacrifices . . . Fortunately there were still some vegetables from Gros Pierre's kitchen garden, but the portions were getting smaller and rarer all the time. We children might complain at mealtimes, but as soon as we left the table we didn't think about it anymore. The grown-ups seemed a great deal more preoccupied. Robert, the cook, who had always been so reserved and shy, was forever losing his temper now, shouting and arguing with Henri.

With the Binet brothers I no longer talked a lot about our escape plans. In fact, I had more or less fallen out with them, because they hadn't even tried to find their father. If I wanted to talk about the situation in Europe it had to be with Philippe—who didn't know as much as Arnold did, but he managed to share some news he found God knows where—or with pretty Rolande who never abandoned her optimism, in spite of her fear.

One evening in August I was talking with Rolande when we saw Gros Pierre go by with a shovel in one hand and his rifle under his arm. We were surprised, and decided to follow him discreetly. Other children joined in. Gros Pierre looked really strange, he didn't turn around even once. When he reached the end of the courtyard, he stopped in front of the orphanage's two dogs, which were tied to a stake. Before we even had time to grasp what was happening, Gros Pierre lifted his rifle, took aim, and fired at Voyou, the bigger of the two. The dog fell to the ground. He was wounded, but not dead. He howled and struggled and tried to get to his feet. Gros Pierre took aim again and pulled the trigger. He had to repeat the maneuver several times, then do the same with the second dog, Grisou, who was not about to submit and let his short life end in such a stupid way. No matter where Gros Pierre aimed his gun, there was nothing for it: the dog seemed invincible. In the end he finished him off with the shovel and his own feet. All the while I was screaming, and the others as well, but none of us dared go near the gardener, with his terrifying eyes. It was neither anger nor rage you could see there, but rather a sort of disgust mingled with resignation.

Once Voyou and Grisou were dead, Gros Pierre began to dig a grave for them, quickly, not stopping a single time. We stood there watching him. Silence. He tossed the two animals into the hole, covered them over, and then finally he looked at us.

"That's how it has to be. You have no idea how much food those animals need. And it won't get any easier when the war starts. That's just how it has to be."

And he walked away.

The next morning, before breakfast, I heard shrill cries coming from the garden. I hurried outside. I found a little group of children at the spot where Gros Pierre had buried the dogs the day before. They seemed both frightened and excited.

I went closer . . . Two huge dog's paws were sticking out of the ground! Grisou's paws. I could see Rolande from where I stood, her face buried in her hands. Other children were screaming or in tears. As for me, I was furious. Those hard paws sticking out of the ground aroused all the anger that had been simmering in me since the day before. I was certain that the order to kill the dogs had come from Henri. Supposedly for our good, so that we could have more to eat, but we all knew that he never liked those dogs and that he often shouted at them. And as usual, he hadn't asked anyone for their opinion.

My eyes met Philippe's. We were of one mind: we had to do something, we could not let such an act go unpunished. Philippe had already been talking with some of the older kids, and they too were disgusted by what Henri had done, so they had decided to go on a hunger strike. I liked the idea, even though I knew that I didn't have a lot of willpower in that respect.

"The main thing is that all of us have to participate. There's not much time left until breakfast. I'll go and speak to the kids who are still outside, and you wait at the entrance to the refectory and tell the others as soon as they start to arrive."

"Good idea. There are bound to be two or three who won't join in, and we already know who they are, but it doesn't matter, thirty or more children on a hunger strike, that's enough to send them into a panic, for sure."

In the end, at breakfast all the children refused to eat. The owl wasn't there, I don't know if he ate in bed or what, but of all those children present, not a single one dared to defy the mobilization order. We didn't even have to intimidate anyone, the importance of the cause was enough to convince them all.

When Henri came to ask us for an explanation, there was confusion, everyone had their own version, some of us demanded he buy more dogs, others that Gros Pierre be dismissed. Before long Philippe stood up and waited for things to calm down. His confident and determined manner quickly imposed silence.

"The children of L'Avenir Social have unanimously decided to go on a hunger strike until they obtain compensation for the crimes committed yesterday, the villainous murder of the two dogs, Grisou and Voyou. The strike, which began this morning, August 16, 1939, will be unlimited in nature."

Henri's face went purple, and his lips were pinched.

"And could you explain to me what you mean by compensation? Do you want us to buy more dogs?"

"We want to be taken seriously. The decision to go on a hunger strike was not made lightly, and we know the possible consequences of such an act. We want to see the representatives of the CGT in Paris."

Henri was fuming. He raised his eyes to the sky and walked away, not adding anything. As we had nothing to do there and the kitchen smells were a terrible taunt to our stomachs, we went out into the yard. The atmosphere was solemn. Little groups formed, children speaking among themselves, and some of them questioned Philippe's authority, whether he had the right to speak on behalf of the others; then there were some children who were proud of the composure he had shown in answering Henri.

At lunchtime, a few of us stood outside the refectory doors to talk with any eventual strikebreakers. But not a single child dared to venture into the lair filled with mouthwatering smells.

In spite of the hunger that made my belly rumble, I found it easy to be on strike. I pictured myself as a knight heading off to conquer enemy territory, never letting hunger get in the way of his mission. I recalled my Aunt Karolka, too, the determined air she had kept about her in prison. The sudden appearance of her face in my mind was overwhelming. I tried to prevent other images from surfacing, but it was as if I couldn't control anything anymore. Fruzia was there smiling at me, and Hugo, too, doubled over with laughter because I had bitten the policeman. I wanted to tell them about our hunger strike, I wanted them to see me as I was just then, so that they would be proud of me. Then it was Emil's turn, whom I had always thought of as a revolutionary. If he was truly my father, that meant I had revolutionary blood in my veins. I must not yield. I just hoped that the people from the CGT would arrive soon, because I knew that our immediate future depended on them.

Suppertime went by. Once again, everyone stood fast. We were beginning to prepare ourselves for the idea of sleeping on an empty stomach. Suddenly Louis came running into the courtyard where we had set up our headquarters.

"I saw some cars, with people in them, and Henri went to meet them, I think it's them!"

Louis had just shouted the news when we saw a strange man and woman walking toward us. Henri wasn't with them. The woman, who had very short ginger hair, walked up to us.

"Hello, we're the representatives of the CGT, which oversees L'Avenir Social. We came as quickly as we could when we heard what was happening. We want to talk it over with you. I imagine you have good reasons for deciding to go on strike. I heard your director's version, and now I'd like to hear yours."

"I can explain the situation. Last night—"

"Could you start by telling us who you are?"

"My name is Jules, I'm nine years old."

"We're listening, Jules."

"We had two big dogs, Grisou and Voyou. And we liked them a lot. Last night, Gros Pierre shot and killed them before our eyes and buried them. This morning, Grisou's paws were sticking out of the ground and some of the children were crying. Henri was the one who gave the order to kill the dogs. He didn't say anything to us beforehand. He didn't even ask us our opinion. He never asks us our opinion, he runs this place like a dictator, he has no consideration for the children. We want his immediate dismissal. All the children here have agreed not to eat anything as long as this fascist is at the head of L'Avenir Social."

"Is that all?"

"My name is Philippe and I'm thirteen. I'd like to add that while we are aware that there were difficult decisions to be made, given the times we are living in, we would nevertheless have liked to be included in the decision process. The carnage could certainly have been avoided if our opinions had been taken into account, and if we had been allowed to suggest some more creative solutions."

"Thank you very much for your explanations. We'll go back to Paris now, and pass on your demands to our superiors."

Long after the people from the CGT had left, my heart was still pounding. I was very proud of myself, for having dared to speak up like that before strangers. I had no more doubts about my ability to become a true revolutionary. Rolande came up to me, smiling. I thought I could see admiration in her eyes. Which didn't help to ease the pounding of my heart.

The next morning we learned that Henri had handed in his resignation. The news was greeted with a great shout of victory and everyone ran to the refectory. Breakfast was a chaotic and joyful affair. We threw bits of bread from one table to the next, sang revolutionary songs, and nobody went on sitting for long in the same place . . . and of course everybody devoured the meal, however ordinary it was, that was set down before us.

CHAPTER 17
Departure

We were at war. The Germans attacked Poland. France and England declared war on Germany. And Arnold and Geneviève were not there to explain what was happening. I felt very alone, and I didn't understand a thing. It would seem that our friend, the Soviet Union, had signed a nonaggression pact with Hitler. But Germany and the USSR wanted to divide up several countries. We spoke a lot about the situation, but nobody, not even Philippe, or any of the older kids, had even an inkling of an explanation. Maybe it was a strategy. One thing was clear, we didn't know what to think or to want, other than a quick end to the war.

And one day everything fell apart. Albert, the secretary at L'Avenir Social, came to inform me that Lena was coming to visit. I was in the middle of playing dodgeball, and the arrival of this woman I was now obliged to view as my mother was never exactly a source of delight. I had long ago given up any hope of ever getting any interesting presents from her. At least she didn't come too often, so I agreed to receive her. She was waiting for me in the dormitory.

When I got there, she was folding my clothes and putting them in a suitcase.

"What are you doing?"

"Hello, my little Julek, how are you?"

She spoke French now, with a fairly indefinable accent, but she still called me by my Polish first name, and that annoyed me.

"I asked you a question!"

"Yes, my dear, I know. Listen, you have to come and live with me in Paris. They are going to close L'Avenir Social. The other children are going to leave too, either with their parents, or to a holiday camp. But you are coming with me."

"And why can't I go to the holiday camp?"

"I'll explain later, we have to hurry, the bus is coming in fifty minutes."

"Are you crazy or what?"

Lena looked at me in a way that made it clear there was no room for discussion. And that is how in less than an hour I was made to leave the life I had known for almost four years. All the children came to say goodbye. Rolande threw her arms around me, sobbing. Roger and Pierre came running just as we were about to go through the gate and leave the property. Roger could not speak. Even Philippe seemed upset to see me go. As for me, I didn't know what to think. I wasn't crying. And yet I was very sad. But there was a war on, and I understood that whatever I might be feeling was of no importance.

PART TWO

I had a new life: wartime Paris. After she came to get me at L'Avenir Social, Lena took me back to 9 rue Aubriot, in the fourth arrondissement. Her apartment was tiny, very dark, with Turkish toilets on an outdoor landing. It was on the fifth floor of a building located in the rear courtyard of another building, and it gave onto a tiny little street that I could cross in two long strides.

With Lena, things were very simple: we spoke when we had something specific to say, she let me do almost anything I wanted, but when she did forbid me from doing something, I had to obey and not ask any questions. Even though she was very active in politics and also, I suspect, in clandestine work, we never referred to it. Sometimes she would run into someone in the street, as if by chance, and I had to stand to one side to let them talk. It never took very long.

I went to school on the rue Moussy, five minutes from our house, with my gas mask dangling from my belt, like the other kids. We had been warned: it was not a toy, nor a disguise . . . Every day I wondered if this would be the day when at last I would have to use it. Whenever I thought about it, I got all cold in my belly and I had trouble breathing. I don't know if it was from excitement or fear. Or maybe both.

I didn't like school. It was too serious. Monsieur Francheteau, our teacher, was very strict. He looked down on us, as if we were inferior beings that had to be trained by making us learn a whole bunch of stupid things by heart. He was always exasperated by the extent of our ignorance. In my opinion, he underestimated us. I sometimes thought I ought to make more of an effort. But any desire to do so faded very quickly. My grades were not bad, but not great either. In any case, there were other things to worry about besides my report card.

The children from L'Avenir Social went to a holiday camp in Royan, or to their parents', the ones who had parents, that is. Rolande gave me the address of the camp so we could write. I told her about my new life: the gas masks, Monsieur Francheteau (I drew his picture in the letter, with a big nose and big ears), and the other kids in the class, but there weren't many interesting things to tell her. I asked her to send her news. And I made a confession, a sort of declaration I won't go into here. Then I waited for a reply. Every day I asked Lena if there was a letter for me. And every day she said no, seeming more and more exasperated. One evening, just before bedtime, Lena's face lit up.

"Ah, yes, your letter. You got one. Now, where is it?"

I focused all my efforts on not looking excited. I think it was a waste of time, because I could feel my ears burning and I couldn't keep from blinking. My mother was too busy looking for the letter to notice. When eventually she found it, it was all I could do not to snatch it from her hand. And I left the room: reading it in front of her was out of the question.

Once I was outside, I crouched down against the wall of the church of the Blancs-Manteaux and set about opening the envelope. I tried to remain calm as the envelope resisted my assault. Finally, I managed to get the letter out. My heart was beating fit to burst. I began reading. Rolande told me about the camp, and which children from the AS were there. None of the instructors had gone with them to Royan. She described the beauty of nature, and the seaside, and she added that in spite of everything she was bored. There, I stopped reading; the dull pounding of my heart made me lose my concentration.

I stood up and took a few steps, breathing slowly the way Geneviève had suggested I do whenever I got agitated. Then I went on reading. After that, nothing but banalities. Rolande sent me her greetings and wrote that she hoped to see me again someday. Not a word about my declaration! No reference to it at all! No answer! And yet she had been truly weeping in my arms when I left L'Avenir Social. I didn't dream it. I really could not figure out what girls were about.

Geneviève and Arnold often came to visit us on the rue Aubriot. They were friends with Lena now or, at least, comrades-in-arms. They no longer hid the fact that they were in love. So much so that Geneviève had a baby in her belly. Well, that is, she used to have one, but she lost it. Of course I knew nothing about these things, but Geneviève explained it all to me: she and Arnold held each other very very tight, all naked, and after that a tiny baby began to grow in Geneviève's belly, because of the seed that Arnold had sown inside her. In the beginning it had been a bit like a flea. Then a strawberry. Then it kept on growing, but one day there was some blood that came out of Geneviève's belly and the baby came out with it. And because it was too small to live outside her belly, it died, or rather she did, because her name was Mireille. I listened to the adults talking about this business, and they all seemed to think that because of the war it was for the best. But I could see that Geneviève's eyes were still sad when she said that. I asked her why, and she explained that even though she was resigned, her heart, of which her eyes were the mirror, was not so easily resigned.

Arnold knew how things worked, where gas and electricity came from, how the radio sent signals, and all sorts of fascinating things. As for Geneviève, she knew what was good and what was bad, how you should behave, the questions you should ask yourself. This was reassuring because we learned vital things with her, without ever feeling stupid for not having known them before. And I think she thought of me as a good person. So much so that one day she looked me right in the eyes and asked me if I wanted to carry out a mission for "us," without saying exactly what it was about. If Geneviève asked me something, I said yes, no matter what. But I acted as if I had to think it over.

"Well, that depends, what sort of mission is it?"

"You'll have to take a document to someone."

"I suppose it's dangerous."

"A little bit, but no one will suspect a kid your age. I only want you to agree if you feel comfortable, otherwise we'll find someone else."

Well, sure, hey, as if I would want them to find someone else!

"When?"

"As soon as possible."

And thus I find myself carrying out my first (and last) wartime mission. I am given an envelope in a bag. I memorize the address of the place I have to go. And off I go, into the blue, into the streets of Paris.

The air is cool. I'm not nervous, just a bit excited, and above all very focused. All my senses are on the alert, I notice the houses, the people, the sounds . . . I walk quickly, to the rhythm of the music playing in my head, a sort of military march. I get the impression that passersby are turning around to look at me and that they are impressed with what they see. A Parisian street urchin on a mission for a great cause. I know it would be better if it wasn't obvious, that I should go by unnoticed, that I should blend into the crowd. But I can't help my piercing gaze and my determined steps.

Given the special nature of my task, you will understand that I cannot record the address where I am expected, nor my itinerary to get there. Here I am. I knock on the door. The sound of footsteps getting closer. "Who's there?" "It's Marco, I've come to see if Paul is there," I reply, according to Geneviève's instructions.

They open the door. I go into a dirty little room, with stuff everywhere, mountains of boxes piled everywhere, which have made corridors that you can hardly get through. I see two gentlemen, the one who opened the door to me and who replied, as agreed, that Paul has gone to play in the park, and another one, with a hat; unlike the first man, he is very well dressed. I hesitate . . . Although Geneviève has prepared me very well, she didn't tell me another man would be there. While I go on inquiring about "Paul," my mind is racing. And I eventually tell them that I will go and find Paul in the park, goodbye, thank you, and off I go, back to the rue Aubriot.

This time I walk even more quickly, I am worried and I am in a hurry to tell Geneviève everything. And when I stand before her, I hand her the envelope. She looks at me, astonished.

"You didn't give him the envelope?"

"No, I thought it would be better if I didn't."

"Why not?"

"Because the man I was supposed to give it to, he wasn't alone, there was another man there you didn't tell me about. I thought it might be someone who was trying to trick him, so I went away again."

"And what did the other man look like?"

"Well, he was very tall, with dark skin, and a gray beard. He was very well groomed."

Silence. I am afraid I may have let Geneviève down. Finally, she bursts out laughing, gives me a hug and says, "You are a great militant, my Julot. You did that very well. But the gentleman was there precisely to take the envelope. So now off you go again, run back there as fast as you can."

I never knew I could run so fast for such a long stretch. Mission accomplished.

Geneviève never gave me any others, but she assured me it was only because it was out of the question to use a child on a regular basis, and not because I had almost botched the first one. She even told me I had acted very intelligently, that I had proved I had great presence of mind. I'm not so sure . . .

Many years later, after the war, Geneviève would tell me that "the man with the gray beard" was the head of their network, and he was waiting for the other man to print up copies of the tract I had brought them. This was one of the wartime anecdotes that were handed down to posterity in the family. And which Geneviève would never tire of telling.

L ena couldn't keep me at her place anymore. As usual she gave no explanation, but I concluded that it was because of her activities that she preferred to send me away for a while. She took me to stay with Roman and Genia—the first of a long list of people who would take me in during the war—a Polish couple, Communist Jews. That gave us a few things in common.

Roman and Genia were very nice. They lived opposite the Parc Montsouris and they let me go there on my own whenever I wanted. I loved walking around in the park; it reminded me of the orphanage, the vast property with its tall trees and birds. They lived in a big villa. From my room I couldn't hear Roman coughing at night. He had tuberculosis. He had to be careful always to cough or spit into a handkerchief so that his saliva wouldn't fly about all over the place. And we had to stand back at a distance when he spoke. As the living room was big, Roman would lie there on the sofa, and I would sit on a bench at the other end of the room to listen to him.

This brief period in my life was marked by the air raids. They began with wailing sirens, rhythmic waves of long ascending sounds. Then silence . . . the air raid was under way. Finally a long note would sound, announcing the end of the raid. And even though they occurred regularly, I was always afraid. During the raids Roman would talk to me. About all sorts of things that had nothing to do with war. I could see it was a trick to keep me calm, but it worked. He was so interesting that I had to concentrate not to miss anything, so I forgot all about the sirens.

One of his favorite subjects was relations between men and women. He said it was important always to respect women. That seemed to make sense, but I decided I would wait to find out exactly what that implied before making up my mind once and for all.

Roman was also passionate about inventions. He told me about all sorts of things that didn't exist yet, such as this very powerful bomb, more powerful than anything anyone had ever seen, and which he called an atomic bomb. What made it explode was nuclear fission, and Roman explained the principle to me, but it was sort of complicated. Another invention, that he was awaiting impatiently, was a box where you could see moving images from your home. Movies, or people speaking, a bit like on the radio, but with the pictures.

Roman had a huge library, and he lent me book after book. Once I finished reading something, he'd ask me to share my impressions with him. For my tenth birthday he gave me *20,000 Leagues Under the Sea,* by Jules Verne, and it became my favorite book. It's a very fat book. I could lose myself in it for hours, because I wasn't going to school anymore—it had become too complicated to sign me up at a third school in the middle of the same school year. Roman had read all of Jules Verne in Polish when he was young. I intended to do just the same, but in French. Roman was really very talkative, so it was lucky that I was interested.

1940 began with a spell of polar cold. I don't know whether it was that or fear of the Germans that compelled Roman and Genia to move to the south, but what I do know is that I had to move back in with Lena. It was freezing in the room on the rue Aubriot.

I went back to school on the rue Moussy, in Monsieur Francheteau's class, and he didn't like me any better than before. So I kept my mouth shut and looked out the window. With the other pupils things were okay, even though some of them called me a Polack and laughed at me. I didn't react. At the age of ten I knew that if there were children who pissed me off I must refrain from jumping on them and hitting them like a crazy man. At recess I would melt into the mass of kids playing hide and seek, and time passed quickly. But as soon as I was back in the classroom, the hours seemed to drag on forever, almost as if the clock hands were stuck.

At home I often heard Geneviève and Lena talking about the Germans: they were getting closer to Paris. One time they were talking about what they should do with me. As I hadn't stopped writing to Rolande, I came up with a plan. She was still with the other children from L'Avenir Social at the holiday camp in Royan. She hadn't responded to my declaration, but she wrote to me often, and every time she said how much I would like it there at the holiday camp.

I set my plan in motion. Rolande wrote to me with the name and address of the organization in Paris which ran the camp. There they explained that I'd have to have my mother's written permission to go to the camp. When I first broached the subject with Lena, she seemed reluctant.

Then one day, on June 13, to everyone's surprise, Paris was declared an "open city." In other words, it was being abandoned, given up without a fight! This was terrible news, and I was devastated, but in my case the tragedy had a good side. Lena's situation was likely to become more difficult. So I told her about my plan: if I went to join the other children at the camp, she wouldn't have to worry about me. Once I saw that she was actually considering it, I pulled out all the stops: "And anyway, all the children are being evacuated from Paris. And there are loads of kids from my orphanage there, so I'd be really at home, and safe, and you could go on with your activities without worrying about me." Eventually she gave in.

A few days later I left the house together with Lena and Geneviève heading toward the Gare d'Austerlitz. Paris was chaos. Everybody wanted to get out, there were people pulling carts, others rushing in every direction, and airplanes—German, French, it was hard to tell—were flying over the city. Geneviève and Lena held my hands and hurried me through the streets, practically dragging me. When we got to the station, the train doors were already closed, and the platform was so crowded, it was practically impossible to walk down it. Lena and Geneviève didn't seem to know where to go. Finally Geneviève cried out, "This is the carriage for the holiday camp!" At the same time, we could hear them blowing the whistle for the train. I was hoisted off the ground and shoved through the window into the carriage. By the time I could wave to Lena and Geneviève they were already tiny.

There were a dozen or so children in the carriage. And two women, Lisette and Suzanne. Some of the children were sad, others were frightened or seemed lost. I was delighted. I loved traveling by train, and I was eager to see Rolande and all my friends again. It was as if I had come back to life after the long Parisian winter. I sat down where Suzanne showed me to and I took a fine book from the *Bibliothèque verte* collection out of my bag, *In Search of the Castaways*, by Jules Verne.

The train kept stopping, sometimes for a few minutes, and sometimes it sat for hours without moving, without anyone knowing why, and we didn't dare go out. Sometimes, too, it would stop out in the countryside and we could hear planes flying overhead and the sound of explosions. We would rush out of the train and lie on the ground until the sounds went away. In the beginning I was terrified, because I was convinced my final hour had come. But after this happened three or four times, I was already less anxious and I didn't run as far.

Each child had brought a little bag of things to eat, and Lisette came prepared with a huge bag full of food. When it became obvious that the journey was going to be a long one, she decided to make up a communal bag by requisitioning everything the children had brought and instigating a rationing system, to try and last as long as possible with supplies that were really only sufficient for half a day. I think Lisette wasn't very good at arithmetic, because already by the second day we had nothing left to eat. For me and the other big kids, that was all right. But I felt sorry for the poor woman when I heard her say for the hundredth time, "I know you're hungry. I'm hungry too, but we have nothing left to eat," or any other variant which was supposed to placate the little five- or six-year-old kids, who thought that war was not a good enough reason to starve to death.

On the morning of the third day, the train pulled into the station at Royan. In my head, everything was all mixed up: at last I'd be able to eat and drink my fill, I was going to see Rolande again—which filled me with a mixture of excitement and fear—and I was going to be with all the people whom I considered my true family. I was so happy to have arrived in the place I'd been dreaming about for nearly a year that I instantly forgot the hardship of the last few days.

While we waited for the bus that would take us to the holiday camp, we could drink at the water fountain, and somewhere Lisette managed to find a baguette which she broke up into tiny little pieces to share out with each child. The bus arrived, and ten minutes later we were outside the gate to the camp.

Lisette and Suzanne thought that the most urgent thing was to feed us. I would have preferred to see my friends again first. But as we got closer to a big building which, given the smells wafting our way, must have contained the refectory, my jaws clenched and my mouth filled with saliva. I started walking faster. I was almost at the door to the building when I heard some children shout, "Look, it's him!"

"Quick, quick, bring him a dog or a rabbit!"

"What's his name, again?"

"Jules, but that's not the name he uses when he talks to animals."

"Tell him to call the dog, he should be able to make it come."

All this commotion left me feeling a bit confused, but eventually I understood what was happening: my reputation had preceded me! All during my stay at L'Avenir Social, ever since our vacation on the Île de Ré when I'd befriended the dog, the children had been perpetuating the myth about my ability to speak animal language. And as I never contradicted them . . . Nor could I bring myself to do so now, because it would enable me to befriend the other children in the camp more easily, the ones who weren't from the orphanage. I had only just arrived, and already they respected me. So while I didn't confirm anything, I didn't deny anything, either.

The only children I recognized in the group who ran up to me were the little ones, no doubt more easily impressed by my linguistic talents with animals. They shouted the few words they knew of that language (and which I have re-transcribed here phonetically): "*Tak, nye, guvno, krulik*" (yes, no, shit, and rabbit). I played along and told them that first of all I wanted to eat, and in the meantime they had to find an animal for me. As I was turning away, I caught sight a bit farther along of a girl whom I instantly recognized from her long brown curls. Rolande turned around and saw me. My stomach went into a knot . . . but someone was pulling me by the arm. It was Lisette, who told me that if I didn't come to the refectory immediately, I wouldn't have anything to eat until evening. That was out of the question. So I tried to send a little smile in Rolande's direction, and followed Lisette.

After the meal, they took us to the wooden cabins, where we left our luggage. I saw the two Binet brothers come running, shouting that I absolutely had to move in with them. I was very happy to see them again; now I really felt I was with my family. And they were so happy that Pierre gave me his place on top of the bunk bed. There were no two ways about it: I was really glad to be there at the holiday camp.

I scarcely had the time to put my suitcase on the bed before

Pierre and Roger were begging me to go with them so they could introduce me to their new friends. I would have preferred to go first to say hello to Rolande, but I didn't see how I could explain to the Binet brothers that I thought it was more urgent to see a girl again than to make the acquaintance of some of their good friends.

I met Lucien, a little boy with a dark complexion and a mischievous gaze; Jacques, a tall thin boy who reminded me of Philippe; and Georges—a little on the chubby side, with thick eyebrows and a determined air. This little group took charge of taking me on a tour of the camp, showing me the trees that were easy to climb, the places you could pick grapes without being seen, a little embankment where you could have jumping contests and, the nicest thing of all, which they kept for last: the sea! They warned me that you had to be discreet because normally you weren't allowed to go there without an adult. We walked through the tall grasses and I could hear it getting louder and louder, a rumbling sound that used to comfort me at night during our vacation on the Île de Ré when I first stayed at L'Avenir Social. We climbed the little hill and when we reached the top I stood there in awe. The huge waves, the foam, the endless sky, the cries of the birds . . . The last time I saw the sea there had been no war, and I was under the delusion I'd been kidnapped, and that someday I might return to Poland. It all came back to me in a flash and I had to fight with all my strength for it not to spill over through my eyes. The other boys had already run down the hill, flinging off their clothes, and they had their feet in the water. I ran to join them, undressing very quickly, but I didn't know how to get in the water, because there was no beach there, only rocks. You had to jump, and right away you were in water up to your thighs, as the waves ebbed and flowed unceasingly.

"Jules, don't be a chicken! Come on in, the sea won't eat you!"

"It's just a bit cold, that's all. I'm coming, I'm coming . . . "

I sat down on the edge of a rock, and let my legs dangle in the water. Slowly I slid down, clinging to my rock, but eventually I had to let go and drop into the water. I was splashed by the waves, I could taste the salt. I copied the Binet brothers, splashing, jumping, shouting—shouting all my joy at being with my friends again, far away from Paris, far away from the war.

After our swim we lay on a big rock to dry out so our wet hair would not give away what we'd been up to.

It was only that evening in the refectory that I saw Rolande again. She gave me a funny look. I went over to her, trying to hide my embarrassment. I had gotten used to communicating with her in writing, and I realized that our letters had given rise to an intimacy between us that in her presence I did not know how to recreate.

"I'm happy to be here," I said.

"Yes, you seem happy."

"Well, yeah, everyone seems nice, I think. You must have a good time, it seems more fun than at the orphanage, with all the grapes, and the sea . . . "

"You know, I wanted to tell you that I've made new friends. I'm glad to see you, but there is Clément, who is my best friend."

"Oh, I see . . . well, that's no big deal."

She didn't say anything.

"We're still friends, aren't we?"

"Well, yes."

And she walked away.

I felt there was something wrong, but I couldn't put my finger on it. Later on I would realize that I hadn't reacted the way I should have, that Rolande wanted me to insist, to make her choose me as her "best friend"; basically, she didn't really care about Clément. I'd made a mess of my first little love affair, but it didn't bother me too much, because there was so much to do at the holiday camp.

It didn't take me long to learn the customs of the place. The camp was surrounded by vineyards, but we weren't allowed to pick the grapes, which made it one of our favorite activities. The boys quickly taught me the basics of the art: never pick all your grapes in one place, never leave an entire stock with nothing. And never go to the same place two days in a row. Of course we ate a lot of grapes, but in the long run, you got tired of them. So, we decided we'd try being winemakers. We plucked the grapes from their stems, filled up some buckets, then stood barefoot in the buckets and crushed the grapes. Then we had to strain the mixture through a sieve and bottle it. We lay the bottles down flat underneath our cabin, and every week we would uncork one to taste it. I don't think our method really worked . . . The concoction didn't taste very good, so I didn't manage to make myself drunk. But there were others who did.

Another activity that I enjoyed a lot, and which was perfectly legal, was going to the beach. It reminded me of our expeditions to the canal with the orphanage. We would stand in a line and walk roughly two kilometers, all the way to the sea. We found plenty of things there to keep busy: we smashed oysters against the rocks, observed the seahorses, or caught eels (which we then took back to the chef at the holiday camp). The nice thing about eels was that you could hide one behind your back and then suddenly dangle it in front of one of the girls. Shouts and screams guaranteed!

CHAPTER 21

The Germans Come to the Summer Camp

One day, the war, which had seemed very far away, came to Royan. The Germans were all over the town, and one morning, their trucks, trailers, and wagons showed up in the garden at the holiday camp, and they set up their own encampment. We were terrified. Especially the boys. We had our informers, and we knew that the Germans, who didn't want a third war with France, had decided to resort to extreme measures and cut off the right hand of every French man (and boy). As soon as we heard the sound of the German soldiers' boots on the ground in the summer camp, we ran to hide in the cellar of an outlying building, where we stayed for several hours, determined not to budge from there until the end of the war. Eventually the director of the camp came and found us there. She told us, finding it difficult to hide a little smile, that this story about cutting our hands off was a rumor that came from God knows where, and that we could come out and needn't be afraid, we could join the girls for dinner.

Once we were convinced the Germans weren't going to cut anything off, fear gave way to curiosity. We ate very quickly and as soon as the bell rang for the end of the meal we left the refectory in a great hubbub.

Outdoors, everything had changed. Every bit of lawn in the garden was occupied, there were Germans everywhere, German wagons, German cars . . . I walked around in the middle of it all feeling a little nervous, but above all fascinated. The soldiers were too busy setting up camp to show any interest in

132 · JOANNA GRUDA

us. So we were able to observe them quite openly. Georges came and joined me.

"You know what? I saw a German go into a wagon and I got a look inside. Guess what there was."

"Prisoners of war?"

"Well, no, not exactly. Rifles and machine guns."

"And Madame Bouillon is allowing them to leave that stuff in the midst of the kids?"

"Uh . . . I don't think they asked her for permission."

And before he'd even finished his sentence I realized how stupid my question had been. The Germans were invaders—they didn't give a damn about the safety of French children. Or about Madame Bouillon for that matter.

Contrary to all our expectations, the Germans behaved very nicely with us. Thanks to one of them I even got my first paid job. I was walking around among the German wagons, very slowly, both because it was incredibly hot and because I couldn't get enough of watching the soldiers. One of them waved at me to come over. My heart began pounding very fast. I hesitated for a moment, but then I realized that to run away would be as ridiculous as it would be pointless. So I went up to him, acting casual.

"What your name?"

"Jules."

"Me, Hans. You, how old?"

"I'm ten. And you?"

He laughed and ruffled my hair.

"Me, twenty-three years old. My French is not very good, very difficult. I want to read and write. You know?"

"Do I know how to read and write French?"

"No. You know . . . teach me?"

"Uh . . . Yes, I suppose so . . . I've never done it, but I could try, we can see what happens, I'm not sure I know how to go about it, but like I said, I'm willing to try."

"Slow, slow, please. If you slow, I understand a little."

"Yes, sorry. I've never done it, but I can try. After, you tell me, it's okay, or it's not okay."

"Super! I have newspaper, we start?"

Hans asked me to read a newspaper article. I read the first paragraph. He looked over my shoulder while I read, then he tried, laboriously, to read in turn. Every time he mispronounced a word, I corrected him, he said the word again, and I corrected him again if I had to. And that way, we got through half the article. He seemed delighted.

"Is good, very good. Tomorrow, again?"

"Okay, I'll come back at the same time."

"Here is for you," said Hans, handing me a bar of chocolate.

Chocolate had been very rare since the beginning of the war. And I loved it. Hans couldn't have chosen a better form of remuneration. I hid this first bar of chocolate carefully under my shirt and only ate it late at night, alone in my bed. It was all soft and warm, but what a treat!

And he went on giving me bars of chocolate for each lesson. After a while, it wasn't such a novelty and I began sharing it with my friends.

It was thanks to a square of chocolate I gave to Jacques that I earned the right to some special information: at certain times of day it was fairly easy to climb into the trucks where the Germans kept their supplies. Jacques had already done it twice and brought back cookies and cans of Spam.

"You want to join us on the next expedition?"

"Is there a risk we'll get caught?"

"No, there are times when it's really easy, when they're at meals, for example."

"Okay. Shall we go together this afternoon?"

"Okay. Normally, when they ring the bell for our meal it's about when they are finishing theirs. So it's easy to get out of the truck in time."

All morning I waited impatiently. When I saw the German soldiers head off to their canteen, I felt a twinge in my heart. Jacques came over to me, very cool and calm. I tried to absorb some of his calm. He explained his strategy.

"In order not to look suspicious, you mustn't watch them out of the corner of your eye or seem to be wandering around aimlessly. The best thing is to run, as if we were chasing each other, or to pretend we're playing hide and seek."

"Okay, go and hide, I'll look for you."

Not hesitating for a moment, Jacques ran off. Out of the corner of my eye I saw him dart into a German truck. All I had to do was go and join him . . . but I could sense that my behavior wasn't natural. I tried to give an impression of composure by shouting, "Here I come, ready or not!" but there was no audience to applaud my performance, because now there were no Germans to be seen. I joined my friend inside the truck.

Jacques had already filled his pockets. He was comfortably installed at the back of the truck eating cookies and inspecting the cans of food in search of something that might interest him.

"Go on, help yourself. You mustn't take too much. Besides, we can come back and get more any day. Look, I just found a whole pile of cans of sauerkraut. I don't like it too much, but if you want some, go ahead."

I really liked sauerkraut. It must have been my Polish roots. When I was little, to make the sauerkraut Fruzia used to make me walk on the cabbage leaves covered in salt, a little bit like what we did here to make the wine. That evening, I devoured it behind my cabin, and invited Roger and Pierre to share the feast.

I was in the middle of trying to get my German student to pronounce the sound "un" more or less correctly when Jacques walked by and signaled to me that I had to go with him right away. Hans noticed his little charade, and because he was getting discouraged that he couldn't figure out the difference between the pronunciation of "un," "in" and "an," he gave me a bar of chocolate and said, "It's okay, we finish. Tomorrow is better."

"What's going on?" I asked Jacques.

"You'll never guess what I found this morning when I was in one of the German wagons?"

"You were in the wagons this morning, before they went to eat?"

"Well, yeah, you see the one that is all the way at the end, behind the three trees? The entrance is on the other side, so you can climb in without being seen. I already noticed it a few days ago, and since then, every time I have been by, there's been no one there keeping watch. So guess what's inside."

"Machine guns? Georges saw some."

"No. The wagons with machine guns are very well protected. But I found ammunition! Loads of it! There are bullets, and some sort of fuses, and loads of other things that explode. You want to come and see?"

What could I say? Obviously I was terrified at the thought of going without permission into a German wagon full of ammunition. And it was just as obvious that I could not possibly miss such an opportunity. But I persuaded Jacques to wait until the Germans had gone to eat, which would increase the safety of our operation to infiltrate enemy lines.

Once we were in the wagon I froze. There really was a ton of ammunition. I didn't dare touch a thing, I just stared beatifically. Jacques had a plan.

"We'd better not hang around here. I suggest we take a few bullets and one or two fuses with us, that way we can hide in the woods and take a closer look."

"Are you crazy or what?"

"Look how much there is, they'll never notice anything, for sure."

"Yes, but what if they catch us with it?"

"I've thought of a hiding place. And we'll go and examine our booty during the next meal."

I had already understood, long before, that when Jacques got an idea in his head it was pointless to try and convince him to drop it. So either I refused to take part in his operation, which would show I was a coward—moreover, I might regret it—or else I stopped asking questions and set to work to get it over with as quickly as possible.

When our dinner bell rang, our ammunition was already hidden in the woods. We went back to our cabin and our breathing returned more or less to normal.

That evening, we rushed over to our hiding place. Jacques had had time to come up with a plan for the ammunition.

"I had a good look at the bullets the first time I found them, since you weren't there breathing down my neck. We should be able to take them apart and take out the gunpowder. If we set it on fire, it will burn."

It was incredible, all the things we could do with bullets . . . To start with, we laid down paths of fire with the powder from inside the bullets. We created all sorts of shapes, and watched as the fire wove through the forest, circling, zigzagging . . . after that, we made a hole in a tree, put a bullet in the hole, and then placed a nail directly opposite the primer and hit it with a stone. It made a huge BOOM and the bullet went straight into the heart of the tree.

Then there were the fuses. In the beginning we tried to light them with our matches, but nothing happened. Jacques was trying to find a solution.

"We need really big matches, so they'll stay hot longer."

"Or we can light a few at the same time, but we'd need more accomplices. I wonder how the soldiers do it."

"I don't think it's a good idea to ask. I have an idea! We'll light a fire, and throw the fuses into it!"

"Oh, yeah!"

The next day, I appointed myself head of safety and went looking for a clearing, because I didn't want to risk setting the forest on fire. We hesitated between several places. In the end it was Georges, whom we'd let in on the plot along with Roger and Pierre, who came up with the perfect place: a huge clearing a fifteen minute walk from the camp, which could be reached by way of some very dense undergrowth.

Our first experiment went as planned. We lit a fire. We waited until it was burning nicely, then Jacques had the honor of tossing a first fuse into the flames. After twenty seconds or so, we could hear a whistling sound, and a bright white light soared in a straight line toward the sky, then a huge BOOM made us jump. We screamed for joy. Then I asked everyone to calm down and wait in silence. I made sure nothing had caught fire in the woods, and we listened out for the sound of footsteps. Everything was fine, the operation was declared a success. We decided to keep the rest of the fuses to explode them at night.

That evening, roughly two hours after bedtime, we gathered at the edge of the woods. It was harder to walk through the forest when it was dark, but we were very excited, and even when we tripped and fell we didn't get discouraged. We managed to reach the clearing. Stage one: make the fire. Stage two: wait until it is burning nicely.

"I suggest each of us prepare a little pile of fuses and when I give the signal we throw them all in at the same time."

"No," said Jacques. "It has to last longer. Let's throw one fuse at a time."

"Good idea. So, has everyone got his little pile?"

I saw four heads nodding and eight eyes looking at me intensely. I savored these few seconds where time stood still, then I gave Georges the signal . . . and off we went! He threw his first fuse. We waited for a second . . . A whistling sound, a lovely green line soaring into the sky, then it fell again to the ground. Then it was Pierre's turn, and his was a lovely orange, then Roger, for a white one, Jacques, a blue one, and finally my turn, with another blue one. Then we started all over again: Georges, Pierre, Roger and . . . this time, the fuse flew horizontally . . . and it fell thirty meters from there, in the forest. We looked over to where it had fallen, and as nothing was happening, Jacques prepared to throw the next fuse.

Suddenly Georges cried out, "Shit, lads!" and pointed to the place where Roger's fuse had landed. There was thick brown smoke rising from the bushes. Then flames. We all froze, speechless. As head of safety, I forced myself to react: "We have to throw earth onto the fire!" When we approached the bushes, we heard voices. A German officer came out from behind a bush, looking very annoyed. He was buckling his belt. A few seconds later, a young woman came out in turn, looking frightened, her hair disheveled. The officer was shouting in German, pushing the woman to get her away from the fire, and he began stamping furiously on the bush. He was shouting in our direction. We had no choice but to come forward. I tried to dig up some earth, which I tossed onto the fire.

It didn't seem to do much good. Pierre and Roger stood next to the fire and pissed on it. Jacques and Georges jumped on the bush, like the German had done. In the end, the German officer took his coat and tossed it onto the flames, and finally managed to smother them.

Once the fire was out, we all stood there looking at each other. The German observed us for what seemed an endless time, then he took his companion by the arm and walked away.

This encounter put an end to our first evening of fireworks. But we gave it another try a few days later, then one more time after that, which turned out to be the last time. One day, the Germans caught us red-handed, stealing ammunition. We expected the worst—to be handcuffed, taken away, and shot— but all we got was a scolding from the officer: "Must not to do that, stealing, not nice. You do again, you go prison. Now, go away!"

Georges apologized profusely and thanked him, in a strange mixture of French, English, and German: "*Désolé, vraiment*, so sorry, *danke, danke schön*, thank you, *vraiment désolé.*" Jacques tugged him by the arm: "Quick, before he changes his mind. Don't insist." And we ran off without looking back. When we reached our cabins, we collapsed on the ground and burst out laughing.

A ll good things must come to an end, and that has been truer for me, in my life, than for most. Toward the end of the summer, a lady by the name of Françoise came to see me. She said she was a friend of my mother's and that she had to take me back to Paris. Without a word of explanation. So I packed my bags, said my farewells . . . Even Rolande seemed sad. Imagine how I felt! While I walked away, dragging my suitcase, Roger and Pierre did their monkey imitation. Even when I could no longer see them I could still hear their simian squealing. I wondered if I would ever see them again.

"Are you taking me back to the rue Aubriot?"

"The address I was given is that of a certain Paulette on the boulevard de la Villette, in the 19th arrondissement."

Paulette was one of my mother's sisters. I remembered having visited her a few times. And I remembered being bored. Really bored. I made up a rhyme: "At Paulette's, it's such a bore, please don't bring me anymore," or something like that. I never pretended to be a great poet . . . To my complete surprise, it wasn't so bad living with her. She even made me laugh, with her accent that was just like Lena's; it was as if they had taken French at the same school, right in the middle of the Jewish quarter in Warsaw. And she left me a lot of freedom.

We got ration cards which entitled us to a certain number of tickets each month for milk, sugar, meat, butter and bread. We weren't dying of hunger, but we were never quite full either.

One day Lena showed up at her sister's with a mournful

face. She had bad news: Geneviève had just been arrested. My mind was racing.

"But how, why?"

"You know why."

"But who arrested her?"

"French police. She is in prison."

"I want to go see her. Can I?"

"I don't know . . . If someone follows you, afterwards . . . "

"So what? I have nothing to feel guilty about, I'm a kid, I could be her son or her nephew. And even if someone follows me, I'll just come calmly back to Paulette's. As far as we know, she hasn't been doing anything compromising."

"You're right. I'll give you some fruit and other things for her."

This was probably what Lena had wanted from the start, for me to go and visit Geneviève. She had even put together a package. But first of all she had to play her role as a mother looking out to protect her son.

My first visit to Geneviève was at the prison of La Roquette. She looked thinner, but she was full of vitality. She asked me about school, my friends, what I was reading. I brought her fruit and cookies, and she thanked me warmly. As I was leaving, she whispered in my ear: "Dear Julot, next time, could you bring me some cigarettes? It's forbidden, so you'll have to get them to me discreetly."

Of course I would bring her cigarettes; I was only too happy to have another opportunity to do something dangerous for her sake.

Since cigarettes were rationed, I used Lena's tickets to get some, because she didn't smoke. On my second visit I went back with fruit and little cakes and, hidden in my pocket, two packs of Gauloises. When I got there I said, proudly, to Geneviève: "I brought you *everything* you need."

"Thank you, my boy."

She came closer and gave me a big hug, a tighter squeeze than usual. I took me a second to realize that this was so that I could hand her the cigarettes, after I glanced around to make sure no guards were watching us. Mission accomplished. It might not have been as glorious as my first wartime mission, but Geneviève's shining eyes made me feel as if I had done something truly heroic.

Every time I went to see her, either at La Roquette or, later, at the prison in Fresnes, I would take two packs of Gauloises.

When school was over for the year, my mother and Paulette agreed that it would be better for my physical and mental health to send me to the country for the summer. I would have better food and more space to run around and play outdoors. Paulette thought I spent too much time with my nose in a book, and it was time to see something of the real world. My mother didn't care one way or the other, the main thing for her was that I got enough to eat.

They arranged for me to stay in Volnay, in the Loire region, with some farmers. This time it was a very nice lady by the name of Lise who took me there. She looked serious, even a bit strict, but I liked people who didn't feel obliged to smile to show that they were amiable: they were more intriguing than people who smiled at any old thing.

So at the beginning of July 1941, I found myself staying with Claude and Huguette and their two adolescent sons Benoît and Paul. If the purpose of sending me to the country was to give me a chance to play outdoors, well, it was a flop. I didn't have any time—there was too much to do on the farm. Anyway, I couldn't imagine playing by myself all day long while the others were working.

This was what I had to do: feed, groom, and harness the oldest of the three horses, Picot; churn; gather the eggs from the henhouse; take the eggs, butter and cheese to the village co-op; feed the three rabbits with grass from the ditch; help with the harvest, gathering the wheat; take the horses to the blacksmith . . . I hardly managed to read even two books all summer! But what I liked best of all was that our efforts were rewarded by food in unlimited quantities. Here I could eat as much lard and butter as I wanted! The first days, I was like a cat in a cage full of mice. I gobbled down huge pieces of bacon and eggs, and butter by the spoonful. I think in one week I managed to ingurgitate all the fat I should have eaten for the entire year. Huguette laughed so hard watching me devour it all that she almost choked. She said she'd never seen a more joyful spectacle. And she urged me to have more, and then more after that. And she went on watching me, her shoulders shaking with laughter.

The first time she sent me to the butter churn with a few buckets of cream, she couldn't believe the tiny quantity of butter I came back with. I just couldn't help dipping into the butter as soon as it formed. Same thing when I went to the henhouse to gather the eggs. I'd put two in the basket, then I'd swallow one whole (I'd make a hole at both ends, tilt my head back, place the egg above my mouth and suck in the sticky contents). "Hmm," said Huguette, ruffling my hair, "it looks like the hens haven't been laying much lately, now have they."

After one week, maybe two, my excessive appetite for anything containing fat eventually waned. And now that they could send me to the henhouse or the churn without fear, I came back with acceptable quantities of eggs and butter.

When I went to the village co-op, I was impressed by the range of food for sale, and the prices. One day I came upon some lovely dried cheese in ash that I couldn't resist. I would never have found that in Paris! I bought four of them, wrapped up three in paper, and the next time I went to the village, I stopped off at the post office to send them to Lena. A few days later I received an envelope containing a letter from my mother and some money. Lena wrote that she was delighted with my little parcel, and she'd like to have some more like that. No more was needed to launch me on my career as a food trafficker.

I tried to vary the merchandise. I was governed by the laws of supply and demand. What had been in shortest supply in Paris since the beginning of the war? Meat, of course. Lena would surely be delighted to get some, she could even give it to her comrades in the Resistance. I spoke about it with Huguette—not mentioning the comrades—because I'd never had to buy meat in my life. She suggested we find some live rabbits, and she offered to show me how to kill and prepare them. Oh dear, there was me, the great friend of animals, and I would have to kill cute little bunnies! But I figured I just had to make the best of things.

The next morning on my way back from the village I stopped off at the Bouvier farm and chose two plump rabbits. Huguette would kill the first one, and I would deal with the other one. I swore I would behave like a true peasant and not let myself be overwhelmed with pity for these little creatures who would feed my mother for several days. As for Huguette, her gestures were very precise and she seemed to feel no emotion, other than some amusement at the sight of my face, because I didn't manage to remain as stoic as I would have liked. When my turn came, I took a deep breath, grabbed Lena's second meal by the ears, and imitated Huguette's gestures as best I could: I struck the rabbit in the neck, bound his rear paws, plucked out an eye so the blood would drain into a bowl (blood which would then be used for Huguette's fricassee). My little sacrificial beast shrieked a bit longer than his companion in misfortune, but I discovered I had a certain talent as a butcher. Then Huguette showed me how to dress the animal, and I wrapped it up and made a package that I sent to Lena. Who sent me yet another envelope with more money.

At the end of the summer the Bouviers came to me with a big crate full of apples—pippins—and made me an excellent deal. They looked juicy, and I filled my cart. As I'd be going home to Lena soon, I sent her nearly the entire crate.

But back in Paris I was met with the dismal truth: I would not be enjoying my share of the harvest after all, because Lena had already sold all the lovely winter apples to her comrades—at cost, naturally. If I had known—but I'd never figure her out!—I would have saved a few for my suitcase. But then when I thought of my comrades in the Resistance, who were risking their lives for our freedom, and how happy they'd be to bite into a good juicy apple, I got over my disappointment.

CHAPTER 25
Clandestine

September, 1941. Once again Lena took me in at the rue Aubriot. Paris had changed a lot in a few months during my "vacation" in the country. People stood in line everywhere, bicycles had replaced cars, it was hard to find food, people looked sad, the atmosphere was gloomy.

The first months, I did what I had to do. Even if I didn't particularly like my life with my mother, or school, or Paris, in fact. I would have preferred to be out in the country, not doing any homework, living with other children like in the days of L'Avenir Social. But those days were over, and I wasn't the kind to wallow in nostalgia.

One morning Lena informed me that we had to leave the little apartment we were living in at once. And as usual, she gave no details. I realized it was pointless to ask her anything, because the less I knew, the better it would be for everyone. She would move in with her sister Annette, and I would be safer with Anna, Emil's sister. As she lived not very far away from the rue Aubriot (in the 5th arrondissement, on the rue des Boulangers), I'd be able to go to the same school. I didn't think it was a convincing argument—I had nurtured the faint hope that they'd stop sending me to school—but I agreed.

Anna was the one who had been handicapped since the day she fell under the tram in Warsaw. She spoke almost no French, but she managed to earn her living cleaning house for people. We got along well and every time I wanted to go to the movies she gave me some of her meager earnings. Although technically she was my aunt, Anna behaved like a doting grandmother with me. Which was not surprising, given the fact she had breast-fed my father!

My twelfth birthday came along. Anna offered to buy me two tickets to the movies. I invited François, my new friend, to go after school. On my way out of the building I ran into Brigitte, the concierge from the rue Aubriot, and she stopped me.

"Hi there, Jules. Haven't seen you in the neighborhood in ages."

"Well, I'm kind of busy."

"Look, I'm very glad to see you, there's something I absolutely have to tell you. There's a letter that came for your mother and I don't know if she got it. I don't see her a lot."

"I don't know either . . . "

"Yup, I don't know what to do. I gave it to Monsieur Hurteau on the fourth floor, but then he never mentioned it again, and I thought maybe I shouldn't have. Look, don't worry about it, I'll take care of it myself. See you around sometime!"

And off she went. I never thought that chatterbox was very clever, but this time, she'd outdone herself.

I didn't worry about the matter, because I didn't have much time to waste if I wanted to go to the movies. François and I crossed the Seine, walked to Aunt Anna's, who gave us tea and cookies to mark my birthday, but I really didn't want to hang around because her son Stach was there. He was a pretentious, arrogant know-it-all. He was an anarchist, and he enjoyed insulting my mother for being a communist. He didn't say anything to me, because he thought I was still just a little brat, and he wouldn't stoop to talking politics with me. In his opinion anarchism was the only system that offered true freedom to the people. It was one thing for him to talk and argue about it with Lena. But one time when he was completely drunk, I'd seen him beat up Olga, the woman he lived with. If all anarchists were like that, I found it hard to believe that their doctrine could lead to freedom. Whatever the case, whenever Stach was with Aunt Anna, I made myself scarce.

I made my excuses to Anna, telling her that we had to hurry if we didn't want to be late for the movies, and off we went to the Boulevard Saint-Michel. It turned out to be hard to choose a film. I wanted to see *The Well-Digger's Daughter* with Fernandel again. But François laughed so hard whenever he saw Fernandel's face that he would wee in his pants. And then his mother would get cross. So he didn't want to go to that one. I asked him to choose another film, but the only one he wanted to see was *Snow White and the Seven Dwarfs*, and it had already started half an hour earlier. And anyway, I'd already seen it.

So we stood there in the cold not knowing what to do. At that time of day there were loads of people out and about on the sidewalks around Boul'Miche. François suggested we have a race, zigzagging between people. We would set off at the same time and run to the rue Saint-Antoine, where he lived.

This was by no means our first race, and I knew François ran faster than me, but because I was smaller than him I thought I'd be better at dashing through crowds. Our rules stated that we mustn't make anyone stumble, or cause anyone to yell at us.

We ran for a long time. At one point I thought François had gotten lost, but then I saw he was ahead of me. I managed to catch up with him at the very end, but then I bashed into an old man who grabbed me by the scruff of the neck with unimaginable strength. François was the winner, but if it hadn't been for the old man I'm sure I would have passed him at the finish line.

I left François and trotted along to the rue des Écouffes, where my mother had been hiding ever since she left the rue Aubriot.

Parentheses. To clarify things, I'm going to do what I

should have done a long time ago: introduce Lena's family. I'll just mention her immediate sisters, all from the same parents. There were four daughters. In order, the eldest was Tobcia, with whom I lived for a while before going to L'Avenir Social; then there was Paulette, with whom I lived before my vacation in Sarthe; Annette, with whom my mother was hiding at the moment; and Lena. Why were they all in France now? I didn't know. Their father also had several children from his first marriage, whom I didn't know. Close parentheses.

I went up the steps four by four to the third floor, using up the little energy I had left after my race through the streets of Paris. I was famished by the time I got there, Aunt Annette gave me a bowl of cabbage, which wasn't exactly what my belly was dreaming of.

During the meal I told my mother about my strange encounter with the concierge.

"She is really odd! She stopped me as if she absolutely had to speak to me about this incredibly important thing, and then she went, 'Okay, I have to go.' I've never seen such an idiot."

Suddenly Lena went very quiet. She asked me to tell her exactly, as best I could recall, what Brigitte had said. I didn't see why, but I made a real effort, because I could tell my mother had something at the back of her mind and this was no time for goofing around. When I'd finished, Lena stood up, opened the curtain and looked outside, before saying to me, her tone very grave: "I think that when she came to speak to you it was to point you out to plainclothes policeman. Story about letter is ridiculous. And it was not by chance she was outside your school when you got out. Surely the police asked her to speak to you, so that they would know who you are. Once she showed you, she could leave. Right. You have to think carefully. Did you notice anything, between the school and here? Any signs that someone was following you?"

I thought carefully.

"Well, we played a game on our way here, with my friend François. We had to run, zigzagging between people. For sure if there had been an adult following us we would have noticed. I even think it would have been impossible."

"Very good. Now, with school is finished. You're not going back. We are hiding you here, and afterwards we find better place, farther away from me."

The police were looking for me! That was really something. I had to hide! At the time, the pride I felt was much greater than fear. How many people could brag about being wanted by the police, in wartime, at the age of twelve? It seemed exceptional to me. But I wanted to go back to school one last time.

"Is not possible, not possible. For sure tomorrow they are waiting for you and they arrest you."

"Well, can I ask François to bring me the wooden ashtray I made in the woodworking class? I wanted to give it to Arnold, and—"

"No, you don't ask François anything. Or anybody. Too dangerous."

Annette was in charge of informing Anna that I wouldn't be going back there. When she got back she told us that the police had been by the rue des Boulangers to ask Anna if she knew where I was, and that they told her I was a dangerous, experienced terrorist, because I must have had very serious training to learn how to throw people off the track like that.

In the end, clandestinity is overrated. Lena quickly moved me, and then, a few days later, she came to get me and took me somewhere else, to a really nice apartment belonging to some Polish Jews, David and Maria. I wasn't allowed out, and there were no interesting books, and they were rarely at home . . . No need to explain that the hours were long, horribly long. I was even beginning to miss school! And I no longer had the right to visit Geneviève, given my clandestine status.

One day Lena showed up with Arnold. Even that was an event in my long day. Arnold informed me that he had new identity papers for me.

"Does that mean I'm going to change my name?"

"Of course."

"And do I get to choose my name?"

"No, it's already been decided, I have your birth certificate here."

As he spoke, Arnold handed me a document. I looked down, read the paper . . . I couldn't believe my eyes!

"What? But why? I mean, did something happen to him?"

"No, no, everything's fine, don't worry."

"But why would I be called Roger Binet?"

"It's a little bit by chance. Roger was looking for a little job, he asked me to help him, so I remembered to tell him I needed his birth certificate. That's all. So now there are two Roger Binets."

"I hope no one will start calling me Robinet . . . "

The memory of Roger's nickname made Arnold burst out laughing. Lena didn't understand what was going on. Then she explained to me that she'd found a family out in the country, in Normandy, who had agreed to take Roger Binet in. And that became my next destination.

Y ou take the train to Évreux. That is on ticket, you won't forget. After that, you ask for bus to Verneuil. After is easy, you can walk, you ask for the way to Candèssiritan . . . "

As I couldn't understand the name of the town—given the way Lena pronounced it, it sounded like a Spanish town—I looked on a map of Normandy that I found at David and Maria's place. Initially I couldn't see anything that looked remotely like what Lena had said. I kept on looking near Verneuil . . . and eventually understood: Condé-sur-Iton!

Lena couldn't find anyone to take me there, but she thought that a twelve-year-old boy, who was resourceful in addition to everything else, should be perfectly capable of making the journey on his own. So if she thought so . . .

The train journey wasn't as difficult as the time I went to Royan, we didn't stop all the time, we didn't have to jump off of the train because of the planes, but I wasn't as enthusiastic about the trip, so it seemed endless. My mother didn't give me enough to eat and this time she outdid herself by putting me on a train in the middle of January with nothing to wear but a cardigan and short trousers. I had a suitcase, but I double checked, and it contained nothing warmer. That was where the papers attesting to my new identity were, so I was careful not to let it out of my sight. In the train I had time to rehearse my life story a dozen times.

I was Roger Binet, the eldest son of a family of six. I lived in Paris, in the 20th arrondissement, near the prison of La Santé. My mother's name was Janine and my father's, Maurice. Ever since the beginning of the war we hadn't had enough food and as the eldest I was at an age where you need to eat, so they were sending me to the country to my aunt Olga's, because they figured that there, at least, I'd have enough to eat.

I got off at the station in Évreux. I wandered up and down the platform for a while, not knowing what to do. Eventually I went into the station and approached the ticket office. A man with a haughty air replied, "But the last bus to Verneuil already left! You should have gotten here sooner. The next one is at nine o'clock tomorrow morning."

It was obvious he wasn't in any way inclined to help me figure out what to do in the meantime. Or how I could get some food. My belly was raging with hunger pangs, and I couldn't think straight, all I wanted was to sit on the ground and wait for someone to come and rescue me. But I wasn't a child anymore, so I got hold of myself and looked all around, hoping to see the sort of smiling face that would encourage me to ask for help. The station buffet caught my attention. My mother had left me some change for the bus, surely she would have worked it out so there'd be enough for me to buy a little something to eat and to drink.

I went to sit at the bar. Behind me I heard someone shout, "Glass of calvados over here!" When the waiter asked me what I wanted, I said, "I'd like a glass of calvados, please." He gave me a funny look, then shrugged his shoulders and turned around to prepare the drink. From the smell alone I could see why the waiter was surprised. But I went ahead and took a sip, swearing I would not spit it back out . . . Well, despite the overpowering smell, I liked the taste. And it warmed me up, which in my situation was not to be underestimated. I tried to concentrate on the calvados and not think about the fact that I might well have to spend the night out of doors, in short trousers, in subzero temperature.

A man who was at least forty, also sitting at the counter, turned and spoke to me.

"Well, lad, looks like you like your calvados!"

"Yes, I like it."

"What's your name?"

" . . . Roger . . . "

Phew! In spite of my fatigue and the calvados, I'd gotten it right. I'd hesitated for a second, but that could be chalked up to shyness. And I didn't add my last name, which wouldn't have been very natural.

"And what are you doing here all alone, Roger?"

"I have to take the bus to Verneuil, but there aren't any until tomorrow morning."

"Where have you come from?"

"Paris. My mother got the schedule wrong, so I missed the bus to Verneuil. I don't know where to sleep."

It seemed as if the calvados had loosened my tongue and given me some courage.

"You can go to the Red Cross. They'll give you a bed and some food there. And tomorrow you'll be all set to take your bus."

"And where's the Red Cross?"

"I'll be going in that direction. If you like, I can show you the way."

"Now?"

"Ah no, I have to finish my drink, first. And you have to finish yours."

My legs were beginning to go wobbly from the calvados. The few times I'd drunk alcohol, I'd fallen asleep almost at once. This didn't seem like the right time for a nap. So I ordered a coffee, with a few lumps of sugar, which I sucked on to ease my hunger. The man who was supposed to guide me was chatting away as he finished his drink . . . and he decided to have another one, the last one, he promised. I asked for another lump of sugar. The waiter gave me a whole handful. When my benefactor had finished his last drink, he said thanks and see you soon, and off we went. Outside I did everything I could to keep my teeth from chattering and my body from trembling. Fortunately the Red Cross wasn't far from the station.

The next morning I woke up bright and early. It was still just as cold, maybe even colder, or maybe I was more tired and less resistant. I got to the station early enough to have a cocoa and a croissant. But first I had to buy my ticket. The man at the ticket office looked kinder than the one yesterday . . . but, for all that, he didn't have good news for me.

"There's no more nine o'clock bus on Fridays, hasn't been for ages, lad."

"Yes but yesterday, the man at the ticket office, he said—"

"Yes I know, but he made a mistake, it happens to everyone. He doesn't work on Fridays, so he doesn't know, or he forgot."

"And the next one, when is it?"

"At one o'clock."

I let out a deep breath. I wished I could give it all up and go back to Paris. If I'd known, I would have stayed longer at the Red Cross, where it was warm. I went ahead and bought my ticket. I had enough money for two more croissants and another cocoa. My patience was exhausted—it wasn't fun anymore to sit at the bar, and time went by so very, very slowly.

Time at last. I got into the bus that took me to Verneuil, where all that was left to do was walk to "Candèssiritan." I wanted to take my time, because I was uncomfortable after all at the thought of just showing up like that at the home of some people I didn't know and who had to take me in . . . but I discovered that the cold is an excellent remedy against shyness. I asked a lady who had been on the bus with me from Évreux whether she knew how to get to Condé. She talked about a bus that went as far as Breteuil, otherwise I could walk to Breteuil and from there it would take less than an hour to reach Condé. "You'll see, it's not that far. In two hours you'll be there."

I was still wearing my short trousers, it was still below zero, there was snow, and I didn't have any boots. I wondered how Lena could possibly be in the Resistance, preparing tracts, handing them out, never getting caught . . . and yet she couldn't imagine I might need warm clothes for the trip from Paris to Condé-sur-Iton in the middle of January. The walk was a good deal longer than what the lady at the station had said; two hours after I left Verneuil I still hadn't gotten to Breteuil, and yet, in all that time walking and thinking, I couldn't find an answer to the puzzle of my mother's oversight.

In Breteuil, a sign indicated that Condé was four kilometers from there! It was almost dark. I sat at the side of the road, disheartened, but the cold penetrated so quickly that I completed this last stage of my adventure practically at a run. Ah! I saw a village which had to be Condé-sur-Iton. With chimneys, and smoke rising to the sky. This time I wasn't running, I think I was flying.

There was no one in the streets, so I knocked on the door of a house and asked where the Buissons lived. I had to go down the street, which was very steep, and right at the end, turn right. The village café was on the ground floor of the Buissons' house. I almost expected to be told that there was no one there by that name. But no, these people who were supposed to take me in and feed me and house me, they really did exist.

When I entered the warm house that smelled of soup and roast chicken, and I saw these people welcoming me with big smiles, and running to fetch me a thick sweater, shouting,

"Poor little mite, he must have been freezing!" I was so over-come by a sense of well-being that I would have gladly left the house just to come back in again ten times over, so as never to forget that sensation.

CHAPTER 27

Roger and the Buisson Family

I quickly felt at home with the Buisson family in Condé-sur-Iton. There was Olga, with her gentle round face, framed with very short black hair; Robert, her husband, short, round and blond, reeking of snuff, occasionally a bit gruff but never nasty; Paulette, their daughter, in her twenties, very pretty, with big serious eyes; Liliane, three years old, Paulette's little girl—the father had been taken prisoner by the Germans and no one knew what had become of him; and Mémé, Olga's mother, Paulette's grandmother and Liliane's great-grand-mother. She was all wrinkled, almost deaf, but she laughed like a young schoolgirl with a hoarse voice.

My first evening was spent eating, becoming acquainted, eating some more, and settling into my bedroom . . . where I fell asleep in less than two minutes, thanks to the fatigue from the journey and the heat from a hot brick wrapped in a towel which Olga placed at my feet beneath the duvet. That first night I woke up several times. I thought about my adventures. I buried my face beneath the warm duvet. I could smell the chicken on my fingers. And I thought again about what Olga had said: "Your mother, Janine, is my cousin. I offered to take you in because I knew that she had a hard life in Paris with the six children and that you were at an age where you had to get a good meal inside you. We'll start practicing tomorrow. You have to learn to react in the right way when you hear the name Roger. The villagers have plenty of time to watch everyone and start to wonder about things. Your story has to be perfectly consistent."

Saturday morning. I started my new life. I helped around the house, I brought in the firewood, they gave me newspapers to read . . . and, from time to time, someone said, "Roger," naturally, without shouting, without placing too much stress on the name. It was only by evening that my reaction time began to seem natural. It was hard to lose such an ingrained habit in only a few days. But Olga never lost her patience and she was relentless with her "adaptation exercises."

On the Monday they enrolled me at the village school. I wasn't in such a hurry to go, but Robert thought we shouldn't waste any time and that it would be good for me to make friends. Olga taught me how to lie (something that would prove useful on numerous occasions during the war): never anticipate people, or start spouting everything you've learned by heart unless it's in answer to a question. You had to have all your answers ready, but only get them out when it was necessary.

The day I started school I was a perfect Roger Binet. I had to introduce myself to the class. I said as little as possible: I'd come from Paris, we didn't have much to eat there, so I had come to stay with my Aunt Olga (who wasn't exactly my aunt, but as good as). No, I didn't miss my parents. Maybe one of my brothers, the youngest one. I told them quickly what life in Paris had been like since the beginning of the war.

Before long no one was interested in my previous life at all. I was Roger Binet who went to the village school in Condé-sur-Iton with the other local children, who lived with Olga and Robert, and who helped Olga from time to time, because in addition to looking after the café with Paulette, she worked as the mailman and she needed help delivering the mail by bicycle. And on Tuesdays, after school, she'd ride up the steep hill on her bike with a trailer at the back to go to the bakery in Breteuil and fetch the bread for everyone in Condé, in exchange for sheets of paper covered with the ration tickets all the clients of the café had given her. When Olga first asked me if I could help her with the mail and the bread delivery, I went all red and had to confess that I didn't know how to ride a bike.

"Never mind, I'll continue to take care of it. Maybe Robert can teach you?"

But Robert always had something better to do, or not do. In the end it was Arnold, who had come to see me on a surprise visit for a few days, who taught me. By the time he left, I was ready to take over from Olga.

They also asked me to go with Mémé on Thursdays to collect old dead branches in the park surrounding the old château. There were two châteaux in the little village of Condé-sur-Iton: the old one, which was from the twelfth century, where the "old count" lived, and the "new castle" from the seventeenth century, where the "young count" lived, and where the German garrison had been staying since the Occupation. I pulled the big wagon and sawed the wood, but Mémé was the one who chose the branches that were dead enough so the forester wouldn't mind if we took them. Thursday was my favorite day, because after the wood gathering I was allowed a glass of fermented cider along with the adults.

At school the teacher was called Gérard. There were twenty or so of us boys and, in another building, Marcelline, Gérard's wife, taught the twenty or so girls. In my class there were only four boys my age, who were only there half the time, because they had too much work at home or on the farm to come to school. Gérard was a colorful character, who knew a heap of things; he liked to talk with the children and preferred to let us find the solution rather than hand it to us on a silver platter. I never grumbled when it was time to leave for school. But what made me happiest of all in Condé was family life at home with the Buissons. I had my responsibilities, like everyone else, and sometimes I thought I had too many and I complained, but I had the impression that all of this was "real" life, that it was more like the normal life a kid my age would lead.

Olga was the communist in the Buisson household, and she took charge of my education in history and politics. Robert didn't give a damn, he preferred his rough red wine to politics. Olga admired the USSR.

"In the Soviet Union, it's not like here, where it's every man for himself. There, everyone works for the good of the country and the nation. One of their finest inventions is the kolkhoz. Have you ever heard of kolkhozes?"

"They're farms, right?"

"Collective farms. People work all together, and what they grow is redistributed. By bringing a lot of little farms together into one big one, they can buy huge machines, of the sort you don't see here, and that enables you to do the harvest much quicker and without any loss. One day, for sure, after the war, I want to go and visit the Soviet Union."

"They say my father is there."

"In the Red Army?"

There was a sudden commotion outside. The sound of someone banging on the barn door. Olga's face went tense. I hurried to the window of the café and parted the curtains discreetly, and murmured to Olga, "It's a German soldier."

You could enter the café through the barn. Olga told me to open for him. The soldier came in, staggering, and hardly looking at us he said, "I'm thirsty! I want lemonade! Lemonade!"

"Not so loud, please. Come in first. *Ja, ja,* lemonade, it's coming."

"How much? Can I pay with this?"

The soldier yanked off a medal that was sewn onto his coat.

"Well, no, we can't take that, you need money, francs!"

The soldier gave a shout then tossed his medal onto the floor and began to trample on it.

"*Scheisse!* Not even good enough for lemonade!"

Then he let out what sounded like a string of swear words in German. And collapsed on a chair, his head in his hands.

"You know why I have medal?"

"I suppose it was for bravery," Olga replied quietly.

"We shoot French tank. Big tank. Five soldiers come out, they running everywhere. So I have orders to shoot with machine gun! Takatakatakatak. Me, I obeyed, they say 'Fire!' so I fire. Takatakatakatak! Takatakatakatak! They all die."

No one said anything. The silence seemed endless.

"Bastard! I am real bastard!"

He swallowed his glass of lemonade in one gulp. And asked for a second.

"I am going. But . . . I come back. Another day. Listen to English radio, BBC. In German. Please. Is possible?"

"All right."

"I am Charlie."

"And I am Olga. And this is my nephew, Roger."

"Thank you, Olga, you are very kind."

And we quietly got used to him, and he got used to us. He came two or three times a week, after the café had closed for the day. On those nights, the entire Buisson family listened to the radio in German with Charlie, the Austrian. He was kind, he brought presents, tools, things to eat for the family, shell fragments for me, all sorts of things that he'd picked up here and there on his patrols. I was one of the first to adopt him, and to look forward to his visits. Perhaps because I too was adopted. Olga and Mémé, too, were quickly won over. As for Robert, it took a while longer. The first few times, he stayed in a corner of the living room or went out of the house when Charlie arrived: "Right, I suppose we have to listen to the radio in that Boche language again!" But he eventually lowered his guard and now he often finished the evening sitting at the kitchen table with Charlie. They would share a bottle of red wine or calvados, sometimes in silence, sometimes insulting who knows who by mutual agreement.

One Sunday, Paulette came to invite me to the movies. She seemed in a hurry. I hadn't been in a long time, and I thought it was a great idea.

"What are we going to see?"

"I don't remember the title of the film, but it's supposed to be very good. Quick, take your bike, we have to hurry."

Delighted, I went to get my bike. When we arrived at the cinema in Breteuil, Paulette rushed up to the box office.

"Oh, you know what, Roger, I don't think this is my sort of movie after all. Since I have a few things to do in town, I'll leave you here and come back for you when the movie's over. Is that okay?"

"Well, yes, but you'll miss the movie."

"Oh, you'll tell me about it afterwards, that's all."

That is how I was able to see *The Acrobat*, with Fernandel. And several other movies after that. Paulette didn't even pretend anymore that she wanted to go to the movies: she would buy me my ticket, I'd tell her the story afterwards, and that was enough for her. She always listened to my story very attentively. I knew I was a good storyteller, but it seemed to me that the pictures, the actors, and the music would still be better.

I might have been young, but I wasn't stupid: Paulette was taking me to the movies so she could see her lover in secret! After a few "trips to the movies" I was getting a pretty good idea what was going on. It just so happened that sometimes, when we were in Breteuil, we ran into Charlie, and he always made sure to give me a nice wave. But Paulette always looked the other way. Or seemed suddenly very interested in the pebbles on the path. Her reaction wasn't logical. I might not have known much about feelings, but I knew a lot about logic. When you run into someone by chance, someone that you know, you act surprised. And Paulette didn't act surprised. Even if you don't like someone very much, at least you're surprised to see them. And Paulette wasn't. So I concluded that she knew in advance that Charlie would be there. And that while I was at the movies, they were meeting. And I understood that I had to be fair and keep my mouth shut if I didn't want to spoil my trips to the movies.

Charlie was not the only German who spent his evenings with us. There were two others who came from time to time. My favorite, after Charlie, was Karl, who always brought a box of chocolates for little Liliane. She made him think of his little girl, and he showed us her picture every time. He was a member of the National Socialist Party. He never listened to the radio, he just came to sit with us and take Liliane on his lap. And he talked politics with me. I explained to him that the Germans had no chance of winning the war.

"You are occupying France and other countries as well, so people don't like you. And sooner or later all these occupied countries are going to unite and throw you out. Stalin is the one who will win!"

"Well, if they throw us out, that's too bad, because what we Germans want is to build one great united Europe, where everyone will be equal."

"But you can't make people equal when you've invaded them! No one will let themselves be a part of your dream if you force it on them."

"*Ja, ja*, I understand, but if . . . We have to forget countries, and nations. Europe must become . . . We must make big European community."

"But no one wants to have a community with invaders."

And it went on like that, every time he came. We didn't agree, but I loved talking politics with the invader.

The third soldier who came to the café was Tomas. His

French was very poor, so we didn't know much about him. I eventually found out he was from Czechoslovakia, from a German-speaking region. Like Charlie, he came to listen to the radio, but not on the same evening.

From time to time I had a visit from my friend Arnold. He now called himself Roger Colombier and he was the husband of a certain Hélène Colombier (they were from Alsace, which explained their accent), and this Hélène happened to be my own mother. Sometimes they came together, but Arnold also came on his own. When he did, he stayed with the Buissons for several days, spending long evenings talking and drinking. To the people in the village, we were "big Roger" and "little Roger," and I'll let you guess which was which.

Then Arnold's visits stopped. One time, Lena came on her own. I asked her why Arnold wasn't with her.

"I think he won't come anymore."

"Did something happen to him?"

"No, you mustn't worry. It's in his head that something happened. He left our group."

"He's not in the Resistance anymore?"

Like every time when I said the word "Resistance," Lena didn't answer. But I could see in her eyes that she was very angry with him.

A t the end of the school year, I had to take the exam to obtain my primary school diploma. Of all the boys my age, I was the only one Gérard had signed up for the exam. The others were too far behind, with all the schooldays they'd missed. Among the girls, there was pretty Aline, the butcher's daughter, who also had to take the exam. We began preparing for it already in March. Gérard and Marcelline took it very seriously. There was a huge amount of revising to do: dates, places, the names of rivers, their tributaries, the names of all the kings . . . We had five hundred dates from history to learn! Sometimes I got the impression that my brain was filling up with useless information and that there would be no more room for the things that were really important. Olga helped me a lot: she quizzed me, wrote down the things I didn't know, then asked me the same questions again, over and over, until my answers were perfect. Of course, that left me less time to play or read, but I liked this time spent with Olga, and we also talked about the war, about life—in short, about all sorts of things that were not on the program.

On the day of the exam, Gérard, Marcelline, Aline and I went to Breteuil by bike. I was nervous. I had trouble sitting still; I was biting my fingernails and rocking on my chair. Aline was nervous too, but it had the opposite effect on her: she was motionless and silent, as if paralyzed. There were a lot of children from other villages, and some of them seemed quite a bit older than us. When they called me, for a moment

I thought I wouldn't be able to stand up to fetch my sheet of paper.

I sat down and began to read. This was the composition test, and in the beginning I couldn't make heads or tails of what they were asking. Then I remembered Gérard's advice. I put my pencil down, closed my eyes, breathed slowly and deeply, opened my eyes, and took up my pencil. As if by magic, everything in my head was back where it belonged, I understood the questions, I managed to put my ideas together so they made sense, and I didn't worry about the time going by. After that was the dictation. Then the mathematics test: I wasn't worried about that at all, and I finished before everyone else. And on and on it went: questions, answers, thinking . . .

Then came the time for the oral exams, in the presence of the examiner. Mental calculations, a reading test, and last of all, the one I was worried about the most: the singing test.

"Roger Binet, what do you propose to sing?"

"*La Marseillaise.*"

Silence. The members of the jury looked at me, their eyes open wide, then they looked at each other. I had obtained the desired effect. Ever since the beginning of the Occupation, the Germans had forbidden us from singing the national anthem in public.

"All right. When you're ready."

With a great deal of spirit and conviction I began singing the French national anthem.

Allons enfants de la Patrie
Le jour de gloire est arrivé!
Contre nous de la tyrannie
L'étendard sanglant est levé
Entendez-vous dans nos campagnes
Mugir ces féroces soldats?
Ils viennent jusque dans vos bras.

Égorger vos fils, vos compagnes!

When the time came for the refrain, I gave it all I had:

Aux armes, citoyens!
Formez vos bataillons!
Marchons, marchons,
Qu'un sang impur
Abreuve nos sillons![1]

Maybe I sang one or two notes off-key. Singing is not my strong point, you know. And anyway, I thought it was an idiotic test. What are you supposed to do if you're really bad at singing? Did that mean you might not get your diploma? So anyway, I sang, and I made up for my lapses in melodic precision with patriotic enthusiasm. After I'd finished, ten seconds or so went by before anyone said a thing, and no one moved. Some of the examiners even had shining eyes. Maybe I wasn't so bad, after all!

Once it was all over, all we could do was wait for the results. I was sitting next to Aline, so I wasn't in a hurry. She had recovered her normal personality and was even in brilliant form. She asked me a heap of questions about how I'd answered, and what I thought, and she shared both her doubts and her smart replies. I could hardly get a word in edgewise, but that was all right, I loved to observe all the expressions that suc-

[1] Arise, children of the Fatherland/The day of glory has arrived!
Against us tyranny/Raises its bloody banner
Do you hear, in the countryside/The roar of those ferocious soldiers?
They're coming right into your arms/To cut the throats of your sons and women!
To arms, citizens!/Form your battalions!
Let's march, let's march!/Let an impure blood
Water our furrows!

ceeded one another at a terrific speed on her freckled face, with her sparkling eyes, her hands dancing and waving.

Then Gérard came and said, "We have the results."

"For both of you," added Marcelline.

They were looking at us very solemnly. We stopped breathing.

"Aline, you have come in third for the entire canton. As for you, Roger . . . "

"Yes?"

"You have come in first!"

"Congratulations, we are very, very proud of you!"

"Is it true, is it true, really, really?"

"Yes, Aline, it is really really true. And to celebrate, we're taking you to the restaurant."

I couldn't get over it. I came in first! I was eager to share the news with Olga, but it would have to wait until after the restaurant. Gérard poured everyone a big glass of red wine, and we clinked glasses, all four of us.

"I raise my glass to Aline and Roger. We are so proud of you both, and you are destined for a brilliant future. Bravo for your efforts and your perseverance. You worked very hard, and you deserve your excellent results."

We clinked glasses again. And ate. And talked. About the exam, for a start. Gérard was very surprised by my good grade in singing. I acted like someone who is very humble about his hidden talents, but in the end I confessed that "there might have been something more than talent" that had influenced my grade. My choice of song seemed to delight Gérard and Marcelline, who had to spit out a mouthful of wine when I told her the whole story. We raised our glasses to *La Marseillaise*. And then we moved on to other things.

"Roger my boy, tell us a little something about your family. They sent you out here to get a bit of flesh on your bones, is that it?"

"Yes, my mother thought I was too thin. She said if I didn't eat properly during adolescence, I'd stay small all my life. So she thought the countryside would be a good idea."

"And how many are you, already?"

"There are six of us, and I'm the eldest."

"Oh yes, six! How many girls and how many boys?"

I suddenly realized I had forgotten whole chunks of the scenario of my life. I opted for the easiest way out.

"Three girls, and three boys."

"And what are their names?"

I was beginning to get nervous. I made up some names that I tried to memorize as I went along.

"And how old are they?"

"Well, the second one, Pierre, he's seven, then my sister . . . Rolande . . . she's four . . . "

I was stuck. The feeling of euphoria caused by the wine and my brilliant exam results instantly vanished. I had made the children too young, I didn't know how I was going to fit three more in, already born six months ago, when I left for Condé. My brain was much too soft for me to remember all those names and ages. But I had no choice, I had to go on. Pierre was okay, he was like the real Roger's actual brother, so I would remember him. And Rolande, too.

"Then there's my brother Arnaud, he's three. And after that, the two girls . . . well they're twins, actually . . . Margot and Françoise. They're a year old . . . and a few months."

I didn't know it was possible to sober up so quickly. What a fright I had had! I looked at Marcelline, then Gérard . . . If they had noticed how confused I was it didn't show. They still seemed to be in a very good mood, and I would have been surprised if they handed me over to the police just because I'd done a poor job describing my family. Then the discussion turned to other things, but I never managed to regain the light-heartedness I had felt up to then.

Almost twenty years later I went back to Condé-sur-Iton. On July 14, Bastille Day. The butcher—pretty Aline's father—was the mayor of the village. We were invited to a reception at the town hall. Very official, and very patriotic.

I was sitting next to Gérard, my old teacher, and he reminded me about that whole business, laughing very loudly. He told me that everyone in the village knew I was in Condé to hide, and that Olga wasn't my mother's cousin. Everyone was in on it, but they pretended to believe me. Gérard and Marcelline dined out for weeks on the story of how I rounded out my family of six siblings with twins.

I felt naïve. I remembered little Alain, who lived at Aline's place during the war. Everyone, myself included, knew that he was Jewish and they were hiding him. But it never occurred to me that everyone knew my situation as well. I don't know if they thought I was hiding because I was Jewish or because my parents were communists. It hardly matters. What does matter is that no one, throughout all those years that were difficult for everyone, went to denounce us, neither me nor little Alain. To learn this twenty years later enhanced the already very tender memories I had of those months spent in Condé-sur-Iton.

I also learned that not long after my departure our three German soldiers came one after the other to say goodbye to the Buisson family. It was a moment filled with emotion. They explained that they would soon be replaced by an SS unit and that it was pointless trying to fraternize with them, because they were real bandits. They would have to serve them politely and never, never talk to them the way we used to talk with Charlie, Carl, and Tomas, who were simple soldiers in the Wehrmacht. Charlie asked Robert to give him some civilian clothing, because he didn't want to have to shoot people ever again, and he was hoping for a chance to desert. After the war, no one had any news from him.

CHAPTER 29
The Child and the Orange

I stayed for part of the summer in Condé, living the life of a Norman villager. But I knew I would have to leave before the beginning of school, because I had no intention of stopping school after my diploma, and there was no lycée in Condé. The local children who wanted to pursue their studies were sent to boarding school. I would be going back to Paris to live. This added a hue of sadness to the summer, because even though I was used to constant change, this time I had become very attached to my adoptive family.

Of all the people whose lives I shared during those years, Olga, Robert, Paulette, Liliane and Mémé were the ones I would think of most often after the war.

A few weeks before my thirteenth birthday, the time came for me to go back to my life of wandering, after a painful farewell in Breteuil, where the Buisson family had accompanied me, on foot.

In Paris I went to live with Francine, Michel, and their son Pascal. They lived on the border between the 16th arrondissement and Boulogne-Billancourt. Francine was a tall, calm woman, with little round eyes, serious and gentle. Michel was an Egyptian of Greek origin, and in the beginning his intense gaze made me uncomfortable. But I soon discovered that it concealed curiosity rather than judgment. As for little Pascal, he didn't seem too happy to see me suddenly move in. I tried to make friends with him, but before long I gave up, because my silly pranks and goofiness didn't make him laugh at all.

Like Olga, they were communist sympathizers who hadn't joined the Resistance but were prepared to help those comrades who had.

To start with, I had to enroll in the lycée. It was not as simple as sending a child to the local school in a little Norman village. This time, the school authorities, in addition to my birth certificate, asked for the family records booklet. Francine already had an idea how to get around this. She knew the director of the Collège Jean-Baptiste-Say, in the 16th arrondissement, and she was hoping to use this connection.

"He's a fairly nice man, but he has certain principles that he always abides by. He supports de Gaulle, and doesn't like the Germans, but he doesn't like communists, either. I think if we play our cards right, we should be able to manage without having to produce a fake family booklet."

"Maybe we can stick with my story that I'm the eldest of six children, but change some of the details," I answered, hoping I'd be able to re-use all those children and their invented names and ages.

"I have a simpler idea. As Monsieur Couturier is a Gaullist, we'll say that your father, or even both your parents, are Gaullists, too. I think it would be better to say you're an only child, otherwise it will get too complicated. So your father, Armand Binet, works for a newspaper in Normandy—we have to justify that little Norman accent you have, and the fact that you got your diploma in Breteuil. Since the Occupation, your father has no longer been able to write what he wants, so he convinced your mother to flee to England and join de Gaulle's government in exile. As the journey was too dangerous to take a child along, they asked me to take care of you, because I'm, let's see, your father's cousin. What do you think?"

"That's all right by me. And do I get news from them, sometimes?"

"Let's say that sometimes you get news, enough to know

they're alive. And obviously, they took the family booklet with them."

"Could we change my father's name so it's Robert Binet? And my mother could be Olga, like in the family I lived with in Normandy?"

"If you want."

"I could say I went with them as far as Dunkirk, but then with the bombing and everything, they decided not to take me with them to England. So they put me on board a train for Paris. I could tell the other children all about the bombing, and how frightened I was for those few days in Dunkirk . . . And you, Francine, you were waiting for me when I arrived at the station. What station do you arrive at from Dunkirk?"

"Listen, let's just agree on the broad outline, and as for the details, you can fill them in as you like, but keep us informed of what you make up. The main thing is to have a watertight story, but to never—"

"—anticipate questions. I know. But that's just what I'm doing, I'm constructing my watertight story."

Our plan worked a charm. Monsieur Couturier was delighted to be able to help people who were fighting for a free France.

I started at the lycée three weeks after classes had begun. In the beginning, I acted mysterious, because I figured my parents would have asked me not to reveal anything about their escape. I was evasive: "My parents can't look after me for the time being, but I can't tell you anything." Then I divulged a few additional details. "My parents are in London. They're going to come back, but it's impossible to know when." I had learned my lesson, and this time I would leave nothing up to chance. Every evening before I fell asleep I went back over the details of a story that no one knew yet, adding new details. I knew the names of my grandparents, where they came from, the exact age of my mother and my father. I made up some old friends, and a dog that I had loved a lot but which we had had to kill. No one would ever even need to know most of these details, but I didn't want to have to suddenly improvise some vital aspect of my life ever again.

Several weeks went by before I made my first friend, Jérôme. During those weeks, I had time to devour a dozen novels about Sherlock Holmes and Arsène Lupin, my new heroes. Jérôme and I complemented each other well. He was very good at drawing and he often gave me a hand in that domain. I helped him with composition. He was very small and shy, but my jokes made him laugh and he embraced all my suggestions for games enthusiastically. He didn't mix with the others, just smiled shyly and was quick to blush. With me he loved running, jumping, and having thrilling adventures—something which didn't interest most thirteen-year-old boys anymore: they preferred to annoy the girls, play hooky, or do nothing at all.

The problem with Jérôme was that his father was a policeman. And for that reason, Francine and Michel wouldn't allow me to invite my friend home. I explained to him that my father's cousin and her husband didn't like children very much, that we wouldn't be allowed to speak loudly, or listen to music at their house, because Michel was a writer and needed an almost religious silence in order to write his books.

"I really wouldn't like living with them. Couldn't your parents have chosen someone else to take you in?"

"They didn't have much time to look into it . . . But it's not so bad, because I just find myself a quiet corner somewhere and I read, it doesn't bother me not to make any noise."

"I could ask my parents, maybe you could come live with us, it would be more fun."

"Oh, no, if my parents chose Francine and Michel, I don't think they'd be very happy to find out I'm living somewhere else."

I was proud of my presence of mind. Francine and Michel were not the cold, distant people I made them out to be to Jérôme. While Francine was not as warm as Olga, she was always ready to sit down and talk with me and she practically treated me as an adult. With her I spoke mainly about politics. And while she was a communist, unlike my mother she had a great number of reservations regarding some of the policies of the Soviet Union. With Michel I talked about literature and music. He had me read one of the books he had written, called *Sébastien, l'enfant et l'orange,* and I didn't understand a thing. The story . . . well, in fact, there wasn't really a story . . . There were characters, yes, but as for the rest . . . Michel explained to me that his writing was modern, and that was why I didn't have any familiar points of reference, but that one must know how to avoid the trap of traditional narration in order to encounter language and meaning, or something like that.

Michel also introduced me to classical music. One evening Francine and Michel had some people over for dinner, with a lot of wine, and they stayed until late. Michel asked me to help out, and put me in charge of the record player during the meal. He brought me the six records that made up a recording of Beethoven's Sixth Symphony, the *Pastoral.* My job was to wind up the machine, replace the needle when the sound began to get scratchy, and change the records. I spent the evening at my post, concentrating on Beethoven's notes—or as Arnold used to call him, "the great Bay-tov." And he won me over in the end: as I had nothing else to do, other than concentrate on the music, once the evening was over I had to admit that that Mr. Beethoven came up with some pretty good stuff.

My first year of lycée was over. Paris was still under German occupation, but our life as a besieged population was not very different from life during peace-time, other than the food, which was in short supply, and pretty much always the same (oh, those rutabagas and Jerusalem artichokes!). Fortunately, I was now in a new category. Like all young people between the ages of thirteen and twenty-one in possession of a ration card, I was now entitled to a J3, the best kind of card. I was allowed 350 grams of bread a day (compared to 275 with the J2), and 125 additional grams of meat per week. There was no more milk, but I was allowed one liter of wine a week! That was pretty nice, but still I was always just a little bit hungry.

Another summer, 1943, another departure for the countryside. To Champagne this time. As for the war, there was no end in sight; the Allies had landed in Italy, where they were advancing at a snail's pace. I stuck little flags on a map of Europe to show the cities that had been liberated by the Soviets. I knew there were comrades fighting in secret for our liberation. They were my heroes, even more than Arsène and Sherlock. Somewhere among them was my father, Emil, a valiant soldier in the Red Army.

"How do I get there, to Champagne?" I asked my mother.

"Lise will go with you, remember? She's the one who took you to Volnay."

"Do I need to take warm clothing, do you think?"

"I don't know . . . maybe a few things . . . I don't know."

The train journey went very quickly. During the few minutes we were alone in our compartment Lise explained to me that she often found homes for children from Jewish families and for those whose parents had gone underground.

"When everything is going well, we prefer not to move the children, and have them stay as long as possible in the same place. Because it's not always easy to find people you can trust. But on the other hand, the longer a child stays somewhere, the greater the risk he might be found out. So we try to take the right decisions at the right time, but it's not always easy to know . . . "

"And did you ever . . . did you ever make a decision you regretted?"

"There's no way of knowing what would have happened if we had decided differently. But one time, yes, I did regret it."

I waited for her to tell me more about it. But a woman came into our compartment. We said hello. And now Lise was looking out at the countryside, and her expression was troubling. A great bleakness had settled over her face. In the end, I preferred not to know.

When the train stopped at Épernay, Lise regained her spirits. She took me by the arm and led me confidently toward the bus stop. After the trip by bus, we still had ten minutes to walk to reach the Biniaux farm. Lise explained that the reason she knew the way was because she had brought another child here, Louis, a few weeks earlier. When we got to the farm, we didn't see anyone. I left my suitcase outside the door and I went with Lise to look for the Biniauxes. We came upon Louis.

"Hello, Louis. How are things?"

"'Lo."

"Look, you'll have a friend now. He's a little older than you, but now you'll have company. What do you say? His name is Roger."

The little boy didn't say anything.

"Go on, tell me where Monsieur and Madame Biniaux are. Don't you know?"

The little boy nodded with his head toward the barn. That was where we found the couple who were to take me in for the summer.

"Oh, hello there, Madame Lise! Are you bringing us the new little man? I hope he's made of sturdier stuff than little Louis. Looks more vigorous at least."

"Don't worry, I know how to work, I'm used to it."

"Louis is very young, Monsieur Biniaux," said Lise.

"Here in the country if you're eight years old you've already been working for a long time. My wife will show the new boy where he's going to sleep. What's his name?"

"Roger . . ."

I settled into the tiny garret room that I shared with Louis. With his pale, gaunt face and dark curly hair, I suspected that Louis wasn't his real name, either.

Even by the end of the very first evening there I realized I was not there to have fun. I was entitled to a good meal, but little Louis wasn't, because he hadn't worked hard enough. They made it clear to me that they would give me a hearty meal that evening, but from then on what I got to eat would depend on how much work I got done. I didn't expect this sort of welcome, I thought that the people who took in refugee children were generous and good by nature. But these people seemed to be short on manpower. Louis didn't look at anyone, and didn't say anything throughout the entire meal. And afterwards he went straight to bed. When I went to join him in our tiny room, I tried to start up a conversation, but after a few unsuccessful attempts I realized that he was sobbing into his pillow. And he went on sobbing for a long time, until at last he fell asleep.

I lay on my back. I couldn't sleep. I had never seen a sadder child. Why didn't he want to take advantage of the fact that he now had a companion in misery? I was not too happy with the idea of staying there all summer long. I consoled myself by thinking that if I worked hard, the time would pass quickly. That night I dreamt I was on my bike, going up to Breteuil from Condé. Little Louis was in the cart behind me, lying among the branches of dead wood. Mémé was pushing us, but she kept slipping, so we all ended up stuck in the mud.

The next morning when I woke up I found that Little Louis was no longer in the room. I dressed quickly and went down to the kitchen. There was no one around, but on the table I found a plate with a piece of buttered bread. And a glass of milk. I looked around, and called out. Still no one. So I sat down and ate.

"You finished there yet? Are you coming to work or not?"

Monsieur Biniaux's voice made me jump. I hadn't finished, but I stood up and showed I was ready to do whatever he expected. My first task consisted of weeding the vegetable garden, planting stakes, and removing branches that were in the way. It wasn't a hard job, and not very interesting either, but oh well, I wasn't at a holiday camp now, that much was clear. Madame Biniaux was kinder than her husband, but she didn't say much. She explained quickly what I had to do, and she left me alone with a lot of tools I didn't know how to use. I didn't see Louis all day long. From time to time, Madame Biniaux came to see me to give me new jobs to do. Every time she cast a critical eye on the work I had just done.

By nightfall I was still working in the fields and was hungry as a wolf, because I hadn't eaten a thing since that morning. No one came to tell me I could stop working. After a certain time had gone by, I decided I couldn't do another thing until I had eaten something.

As I came nearer to the farm, I could hear Monsieur Biniaux

shouting. "Lazybones! Good-for-nothing! Who sent me such a fucking lazy kid!" He was shouting so loud I thought his voice would break. And then there was the sound of a slap, then another, and I heard little Louis cry out. I had a huge knot in my stomach, I didn't know what to do, I didn't dare go and see what was happening, but I couldn't walk away again either as if nothing had happened.

"What are you doing here?"

It was Madame Biniaux. I turned around. She was giving me a hard look, then motioned to me to go into the house. I followed her inside, sat down at the table, and started eating. Louis came in when I had almost finished. His eyes were red, and he had trouble walking. He remained on his feet to eat his crust of dry bread.

The very next day I wrote to my mother and told her what was happening. I explained to her that I was worried about Louis, and that I didn't think he could survive an entire summer like that.

I went on working. And Monsieur Biniaux went on hitting little Louis. When I managed to avoid the farmers' vigilant gaze, I would hide a piece of bread or cake in my pocket, and give it to Louis in the evening, in our room. He still didn't talk to me, or smile, but when he looked at me he seemed a bit less fearful.

One day, Madame Biniaux sent me to pick fruit from the tall cherry tree that grew on the side of the hill. She gave me five baskets to fill. Once I was up in the tree, I took my time, eating at least as many cherries as I put in the basket. Suddenly I heard the buzz of an airplane engine. And it was coming closer, getting louder and louder. It was hedge hopping just above the hill. It was an English plane. Farther away, I saw a train stopped in its tracks. The plane flew over a first time, went away, made a circle and flew back over the train. And the same thing all over again: a second circle, and then a third. Meanwhile, the railway men left the train and ran to hide in the woods. Here came the plane a fourth time and then . . . TARATARATATA TARATARATATA! And all hell broke loose. The train was filled with ammunition. I stayed perched in my tree watching the fireworks. After I went back to the farm, for a long time I could still hear the carriages exploding one after the other. And I got told off for having taken too long to pick not enough cherries.

Roughly a week later, when I came back from the fields I found Lise with little Louis clinging to her while she spoke with Madame Biniaux. When Lise saw me, she gestured to me to come as quickly as possible.

"Go up to the room with Louis. And pack your bags, quickly!"

I didn't ask any questions, but I realized this was because of my letter. I stuffed all my belongings into my suitcase, and Louis put his into a big burlap bag. Then we hurried back down the stairs. Madame Biniaux seemed very annoyed.

"You can explain the situation to your husband when he comes back," Lise told her. "And don't expect to be taking in any more children. That's finished. Come on, boys, we're leaving."

I was still in the Champagne region. Lise took me to stay with one of her cousins, who lived in a village called Mont-Saint-Père, then she went away again with little Louis. My new family, the Brissons, included Albert, the father—who was also known as Albert the Pig, because everyone came to him if there was a pig to be slaughtered—Yvonne, the mother, and their two daughters, Isabel and Claudine. At a rough guess, the girls were almost adult. I had a simple life there: I worked a few hours a day, depending on what there was to do, and after that I went wherever I liked and filled the time as I pleased. After my stay with the Biniauxes, it was like being at a holiday resort.

The Jansons, our neighbors, also had two daughters. A grown-up one who was friends with the Brisson girls, and another one, Suzanne, who was my age . . . and who seemed delighted by my arrival. Every time I ran into her, she looked at me out of the corner of her eye. Initially she didn't talk to me. But very soon she began to ask me about myself, and then started talking about her own life. She introduced me to other young people, took me on a tour of the village and the surroundings. I thought that for a girl she was actually rather nice, and she even knew almost as much as I did about plants and animals. One day she came and knocked on the door.

"Hello, Roger! How are you? Say, my sister and her friend are going to the movies, and my parents are forcing me to go with them. I don't really feel like acting the chaperone all evening, so I thought that, since you told me once that you really liked the movies, so I thought that, even though I have to leave in a few minutes, maybe you—"

"I'm coming."

Suzanne hadn't been talking for more than five seconds, and when I agreed, the little pink circles on her cheeks spread to her entire face.

On the way there, I didn't know where to look. Suzanne's sister and her "friend" didn't stop cuddling, and kissing on the mouth, and putting their hands all over each other. I was fascinated, I really would have liked to watch them, and I also wanted to learn something about what you are supposed to do with girls, but I felt horribly embarrassed, and I was afraid I might have a physiological reaction and Suzanne would notice. And she kept talking and talking and talking and looking everywhere except at her sister.

Once we were at the cinema, Marguerite, the older sister, made it clear to us that we had to sit as far away as possible from her and her boyfriend. Which was a relief to me, that way I could concentrate on the film.

How wrong I was. As soon as the film began, Suzanne moved closer to me, just a bit, and then a bit more . . . I tried to act naturally, but I wondered whether I should just let her do what she was doing or take an active part. No sooner had I started deliberating than her face was up against mine and a hot tongue was making its way between my lips. I couldn't decide whether I liked it, but I tried to respond as best I could with my own tongue to the movements of this moist muscle of Suzanne's. I concentrated very hard to stay calm. And to think quickly. I came to the conclusion that maybe it would be all right to put my hand on her thigh. I started just above the knee then gradually moved up . . . Darn, my mistake, she pushed my hand away. I was ill at ease, so I withdrew a bit . . . but then Suzanne grabbed my hand and shoved it under her skirt! Now

I was in foreign territory. I touched the skin on her thigh a little bit, but I could tell from the way she was moving her hips that Suzanne would like for me to explore further. I was worried about what I might find there. But, oh well, all's fair in love and war! I shoved my hand up further. She moaned, but she didn't push me away. I went on, trying to gauge her reaction so I could analyze the relevance of my gestures. I touched the edge of her underpants. She went on making little moaning sounds and squeezing closer and closer to me.

I didn't get to see any of the film . . . and it took me a few minutes before I dared stand up when it was time to leave the cinema. Once we were outdoors, Suzanne looked at me with big languorous eyes that filled me with immense pride. I felt like I'd come off not too badly, and I had every intention of finding another opportunity, as soon as possible, to perfect my new talent.

Two days later I was on my way home with two bottles of milk I'd been sent to fetch at the Maugout farm when I ran into Suzanne. She looked at me, then averted her eyes and walked on without saying a thing. I stood still, not knowing what to do, and suddenly I remembered Rolande, how upon my arrival at the holiday camp she had treated me with indifference, and how I had later regretted my failure to insist. So I went after Suzanne.

"Hey! Suzanne, are you busy? I only have two or three things left to do, and after that I'm free. We could go to the beach. Would you like that?"

"Well, uh, I don't know. Well, all right, yes, why not."

I would have preferred a more enthusiastic reaction, but never mind, I'd have to make do with a lukewarm "yes."

At the beach, on the riverbank, I suddenly felt ill at ease. I realized we would not be able to reproduce the events from the dark cinema here, but I tried to sit near her, so that our thighs touched. But every time, she moved away. I had to change my strategy. I tried to find a topic of conversation that would interest her, thinking that this might make it easier for me to inch my way closer to her, subtly.

"Have I ever told you that I know how to talk to animals?"

She gave me a funny look, as if she had just found out that I was a complete idiot.

"Well, after a fashion . . . in fact, when I was little . . . "

I stopped short. I couldn't go telling her about how I had just arrived in a French orphanage and only spoke Polish! This was the first time I had ever ventured onto such thin ice.

"Well, uh, it was just that animals always came up to me, I even looked after an owl, I had this sort of gift, and the kids in my neighborhood said that I knew how to speak animal language."

"That's nice."

Phew, that was a close call. I would have to learn not to let girls make me lose my concentration. But she didn't seem impressed. While I was hunting for something else to talk about, a detachment of German soldiers showed up, all carrying bath towels. It wasn't unusual for German soldiers to come and cool off in the river, and nobody paid any attention to their presence. Suzanne stood up.

"Well, since we're not swimming, I'm going home."

Was that what she wanted, to go swimming? Why didn't I think of it? Both of us in the water, in our bathing suits, side by side. But why hadn't she said anything? I was disheartened by my lack of know-how with girls. Suzanne had already left, and I couldn't decide whether to follow her or not. Finally, I stood up and got ready to go back to the village. That was when I noticed that the sound of airplanes I had heard in the distance earlier was getting louder and louder. I could make out a squadron of English planes, those famous Black Widows with two fuselages. Someone shouted, "Take cover, quickly, they're going to shoot the Germans!"

I rushed over to a ditch, where I curled up in as small a ball as possible. The crackling began. It was raining all around me. After a while, I realized it was the sound of cartridges falling. I had enough experience of the war to know that if the cartridges were falling here, it meant they were shooting at something farther on. So I stood up to see what was going on. And then, suddenly, it was horrible, terrible. I was stinging, burning all over my body! I looked around and saw that in my panic I hadn't noticed that I'd found refuge in a field of nettles . . . in my bathing suit!

I hurled myself into the river to cool off my body, then quickly forgot my physical discomfort because I saw the most amazing spectacle, courtesy of the Royal Air Force: they were bombarding a train going by just on the other side of the Marne.

Toward the end of the summer Albert requisitioned me, along with the entire family and several neighbors whose pigs he had slaughtered during the year, to harvest the fields at the bottom of the hill by the river. No more holiday resort! The first days, we had to make sheaves with the wheat Albert had reaped and place them in the haystacks to keep them from rotting in case it rained. Then we had to gather the sheaves: you stabbed one with a pitchfork, got up your momentum, thrust it into the cart, and again, stab, momentum, thrust, and so on. By the end of the day, I was exhausted.

Once the harvest was over it was time to say goodbye—I had to go back to my lycée. I was sad to leave Mont-Saint-Père and the Brisson family, and disappointed not to have renewed my experience at the movies with Suzanne, but I was eager to get back to Paris, where I had every intention of finding an opportunity to put what I had learned about girls into practice.

I picked up my life exactly where I had left it. I was in the fifth class, at the Collège Jean-Baptiste-Say, and I was reunited with all my friends from the previous year. I also settled back into my usual habits at Francine and Michel's. So much stability was almost destabilizing. But you get used to everything at that age, even routine.

I had a new friend, Maciek. He took the same route as me, morning and evening. One day I suggested we go to the movies. He had never been before and he came out of this first session with the shining eyes of a child who's just had a trip in a hot air balloon. I became his official companion for outings to the movies and whenever he had a bit of pocket money he would grab me by the sleeve and beg me to go with him.

Maciek was the son of Polish peasants who had come to settle in France shortly before the war. Sometimes he would talk to me, rolling his r's, about his life in the Polish countryside, about the horses he used to look after when he was little, and the mountains with their snowy peaks, and cold beet soup and kielbasa. And there was I, Roger Binet, having to pretend I had never heard of any of that, and didn't know a thing about Slavic customs. It wasn't a very big lie, because other than the few words I still knew of the animal language (*tak, nie, gówno* and *królik*) and two or three very vague but pleasant memories of Hugo and Fruzia, I didn't remember much about the country of my early childhood. Since leaving Poland with Lena, I had been to so many different places, lived so many different lives, that my Polish period seemed almost unreal to me. But I liked to listen to Maciek talking about his past in Poland, and he was really happy to tell me about it, because I was the only one of his friends who was interested.

That year, the favorite teacher of almost all the children in the fifth class was the Spanish teacher. He was a very tall man with incredibly long arms, and he often came in late. To start the class, he always got our attention by teaching us a new "bad word" in Spanish, something he took very seriously. Therefore, *joder, puta, hostia, cojones, cabrón* and *puñetas* were the first words I learned in that language, and years later they were more or less all that remained. Without having to be told, all the children understood the importance of discretion with regard to this very unorthodox introduction to the language.

Otherwise, as far as teachers went, the school had not been kind to us. Everyone hated the chemistry teacher, Monsieur Masson, because he was strict beyond belief and horribly cold. While his attitude meant that his classes were pretty dull affairs, from time to time he had to pay the price for being so despicable: he was the butt of practical jokes.

One day, when Monsieur Masson was walking up and down the stairs in his white coat in the amphitheater explaining some concept to do with the periodic table, little Alfred, who didn't know what more he could do to stay awake, splashed some purple ink at him with his pen. Silence. The teacher turned around abruptly. He stood there, unmoving, for a few seconds that seemed to drag on forever. He stared at Alfred, then walked over to him—probably very quickly, but the images I have retained of this event unfold in slow motion. Not saying a thing, he grabbed him by the shirt and forced him to stand up. Then he motioned to him to descend a few steps . . . and thump! kicked him soundly in the back. Alfred fell to the ground, rolled down the steps . . . and didn't get up. We all looked at one another, not knowing whether we should rush over to him or stay where we were in our seats. Finally, Monsieur Masson went up to Alfred and turned him over. He was all floppy. The professor went red in the face and shouted that we had to help him carry the kid to the infirmary.

Alfred recovered all right, but this incident was fatal to the chemistry teacher's reputation. A wind of rebellion blew through the classroom. After Alfred's fainting spell, Monsieur Masson found it harder and harder to maintain discipline in his classes. As for me, I wrote short stories during the chemistry classes, pretending to be taking notes with the utmost diligence. As I knew that chemistry would never be of any use in my life, I preferred to spend the time perfecting my literary talent. From the time I had started at the lycée, my decision had been made: I would become a journalist or a novelist. Or a bit of both. So science would not be much use to me.

While nobody liked Monsieur Masson, where Monsieur Vidal the drawing teacher was concerned, it was more of a personal matter between the two of us. A personal matter that would also lead to a loss of consciousness. And this time, the fault would be mine alone.

I was not good at drawing or art in general. I don't know why, but between what I imagined in my head and what appeared on the paper there was always an insurmountable gap. And yet I really made an effort. But I think it just wasn't in the genes. And as for Monsieur Vidal . . . well, my handicap just made him laugh. He loved showing my drawings to the entire class, and thought it was great fun to have them guess what I was trying to depict. It was painful. And humiliating. My drawings got more and more slapdash as the year progressed. And Monsieur Vidal derived more and more pleasure from them.

His cruelty toward me was not the only reason for my hatred. It's true, I swear! There were political reasons, too, for we were poles apart. Can you imagine, my tormentor thought that throughout the entire history of France there were only two heroes worthy of admiration: Joan of Arc and Marshal Philippe Pétain. Joan of Arc, the maid of Orléans, I don't mind. She kicked the English out of Orléans, that's not bad. But in my humble opinion, she was still no more than an enlightened crank. And as for Marshal Pétain, he was at best an opportunistic collaborationist and at worst, a fascist, anti-Semitic old man who brought about France's downfall so that he could seize power.

If I've devoted this long preamble to my relations with Monsieur Vidal, to describe the hatred he aroused in me, it's not solely my self-esteem at work. All alone in my corner, I was quietly plotting my revenge. Fairly recently I had started spending a lot of time in joke and novelty shops. And I needed some new victims on whom to test my purchases. Monsieur Vidal seemed the perfect candidate. I hesitated between a stink bomb and a whoopee cushion, placed discreetly on his chair just before class. It would be funny, but I wasn't sure . . . Both were fairly common, and not nearly nasty enough.

One morning I had a sudden burst of inspiration. When he had his back turned I blew a strong dose of sneezing powder at his head. Let's just say I might have overdone it. Monsieur Vidal didn't even have time to realize what had happened before he started choking . . . His lips went blue and he collapsed on the floor in a faint. Silence in the classroom. Followed by intense commotion. And silence again when Monsieur Vidal got back to his feet, stood there for a few moments holding onto a chair, then left the room. We sat stock still, not daring to imagine what would happen next. Personally, I felt sad. My revenge had been more spectacular than planned, but for some unknown reason it didn't satisfy me. And I was worried about what was to come.

For a very long while, nothing happened. All you could

hear in the classroom was some whispering and the rustling of paper. Then the door opened. It was the headmaster.

"Monsieur Vidal has just been to my office. I suppose that what happened to him is the result of a particularly stupid prank. I will not leave this room until I have the name of the perpetrator of these vile shenanigans. Would anyone care to come forward?"

Silence.

"So be it. Well, would anyone care to denounce the culprit?"

Long silence.

"Given the gravity of the incident, I will allow myself to resort to a method that I don't often use. I will give the culprit, or anyone who knows his identity, two more minutes to come forward. After that, the entire class will be punished, very severely."

Heavy silence.

Which I eventually broke, after ten seconds or so had gone by. "It was me . . . "

"Excuse me. Could you speak up, Master Binet?"

"It was me."

"You are guilty, is that what you are saying?"

"Yes."

"Good, good. Then come with me. The rest of you, take out a book, a notebook, anything, find something to do until the end of class. Quietly."

My tête-à-tête with the headmaster was not exactly pleasant. He asked me where I had bought my sneezing powder. I tried as best I could to protect my sources. My punishment consisted of three days' suspension from school and a zero for conduct. As was to be expected, this misadventure did not improve my relations with the drawing teacher. But he no longer dared make fun of me. He merely acted as if I did not exist, which, in the end, was better.

All of this was nothing compared to the scolding I got from Francine when I came home and informed her that I had three days off ahead of me. She was furious! No matter how often I explained that Monsieur Vidal deserved his punishment, and that it had not gone the way I expected, she would not calm down. She thought that for someone who was living under an assumed name with false papers, I had acted extremely carelessly. She wasn't wrong. I hadn't seen things from that angle.

"I hope you didn't say that it was your teacher's political opinions that you gave you such pleasure in causing him to faint."

"Well, no, I'm not that stupid."

"Sometimes I wonder."

Y ou might be tempted to think that it had something to do with the episode of the sneezing powder, but Francine assured me it didn't: one month after my three-day suspension, she informed me that I would no longer be going to Jean-Baptiste-Say, that I would no longer be living with Michel and her, and that I would be a boarder in a little school in Saint-Maur-des-Fossés, not far from Paris. For the first time, I spoke up to protest against this change in my life the adults had planned for me.

"I like it here, nobody suspects a thing, I have friends, everything is great. Why do I have to move again?"

"It's your mother's decision. She has her reasons."

"Then let her come and explain them to me in person. She's not the one who has to make up a new story every time, and always has to be careful not to make mistakes whenever she opens her mouth. I want to know her reasons, and if they're no good, I don't see why I should move from here!"

Francine didn't say anything. She looked sad. Suddenly I felt uncomfortable. What if it was Michel and Francine who were afraid, and wanted to avoid putting their own son's life in danger because of me?

"You know, your mother isn't doing this just to annoy you. I am sure that someday, when you grow up, she'll be able to justify every decision she has made. And that she won't regret a single one."

"But I'm big now, I'm fourteen! Let her come and justify

her decisions, and if it's true she has good reasons, then I'll go to Saint-More-of-the-Fussies without a fuss, and I'll re-re-rehearse my story all over again, or even make up a brand-new one."

"She can't come right now, it would be too dangerous, for her and for us. You have to trust her and not ask any questions. I promise you that you'll understand someday, when the war is over."

Lena. Her maternal instinct was not very developed. I'd had several mothers in my life, and so I was able to compare. And at times I suffered because of it, and this must have influenced my opinion of her. But it would be unfair not to mention her superb qualities as a militant, which were the reason for this new change in my life. Lena was a very important member of the Resistance. She was brave. And intelligent. And extremely intuitive, which is no doubt what helped her to survive the war.

According to what she told me later on, one of my mother's resistance strategies was to always leave the house well dressed, wearing makeup, and perfectly groomed. In France, roundups were generally carried out by French policemen, so it was surely a good tactic. One day she was standing on the platform in the métro when she saw some police officers asking everyone for their papers. In her handbag my mother had some leaflets from the Resistance. Like a shot, she went straight up to be first to be checked by the officers. She begged them, simpering, "Oh please, oh please, officer, I'm in the most terrible hurry, I have a date with my lover, and I'm already terribly late." She went ahead of everyone without even having to show her papers, while the policeman gave her a knowing wink.

I had no choice, I had to get ready to move yet again. We came up with a new version of Roger Binet's life, somewhere in between the one used in Normandy and the one used in Jean-Baptiste-Say. Once again I had fun learning the broad outlines and inventing new details.

One week after learning that I would have to move, I was boarding with Monsieur Barbier, a math teacher at my new school, the lycée at Saint-Maur-des-Fossés. There were about a dozen of us boys living upstairs in a huge house, while the teacher lived on the ground floor. We tried to avoid him as much as we could, this surly old man with a white beard full of tiny relics of his meals.

This time it was the French teacher I liked best of all, Monsieur Noiret. He had us read books we really liked, not just the things "you have to have read in order to show you have some culture." And I found out that required reading can bring you as much happiness as a book you've chosen yourself. Maybe because we didn't expect anything, and we thought we'd be bored to hell. So when, instead, you find yourself captivated, and you become feverishly absorbed in the story, and you keep delaying the time to switch off the light to go to sleep, it's even more intoxicating than with an author you know in advance you will like. Monsieur Noiret gave us novels that were for young people, not children, books that had bad words in them, for example. Like *The War of the Buttons,* which has this sentence I adore: "Fancy-schmancy, super-duper, shit, how amazing," which became the favorite expression of the fifth-year students at the Collège in Saint-Maur-des-Fossés. And there were the shorter versions: "That's fancy-schmancy, super-duper!" or "Shit, that's super-duper!" And of course, a new insult was added to our repertory: "candy-ass."

We were in the thick of the war. It was the real thing, with heavy bombing and all. You could sense the end was in sight . . . and victory. When we were at the lycée and heard the air raid sirens, we had to rush out into the trenches dug in the schoolyard. Sometimes we were glad to have a break, it was almost like recess. For example, there was one time when the English teacher had just asked me a tricky question, and the sirens started up. And when we got back to class and the teacher asked, "Right, where were we, before the air raid?" the others were terrific, no one said a thing. But in the long run you got tired of it, those endless minutes when you were all crammed together in the trenches. So a few pals and I began discreetly slipping off to run and jump in the Marne. After all, we had all learned that the bombing only killed other people. And besides, there was no danger that the Americans might start bombing swimmers! By day, it was mainly the Americans bombing, from very high up, with their immense flying fortresses.

At night, at Monsieur Barbier's, we would go down into the cellar when the sirens started wailing. There too, we began to see how pointless it was, and above all, how boring. So after the first few times, we went to sit rather out on the roof of the house. From there we could watch a magnificent show: the DCA, the antiaircraft defense, lit up the planes with huge searchlights (at night, these were mainly English planes, flying very low) and shot at them; we also saw the fireworks created by the rockets the planes fired to show where to bomb . . . This was a hundred times better than any fireworks display. And sometimes, if we were lucky, the bombing was close enough for everything to begin to vibrate around us. When this happened, it was more than just fireworks, it was like being at an amusement park. In Saint-Maur-des-Fossés, during this period near the end of the war, we were rarely bored.

On Saturdays I went back to Paris. I would take the train as far as the Bastille, and from there I walked to Lena's house (Madame Hélène Colombier) on the passage Montgallet in the twelfth arrondissement. I didn't have any friends in the neighborhood, so I took a lot of reading along.

I also spent Easter vacation at Lena's. One evening, looking very distraught, she told me that Saint-Maur-des-Fossés had been bombed! I immediately wondered whether the school had been hit and whether we'd have a long vacation. Imagine, what a thing to think . . . Naturally I soon realized that there might be people I knew among the wounded or the dead . . . but nearly all the students had left town for the vacation, and the teachers . . . Of course I'd be sad if any of the teachers had been killed . . . But if the school had been hit during the bombing raid and we had a nice long break, that wouldn't be bad at all!

Except there are the things you imagine and there's reality. The school wasn't even remotely hit, and we went back to class on Tuesday morning as if nothing had happened. In the days that followed, we heard on the BBC that the bombing in Saint-Maur was an error which the Allies "sorely regretted" . . . As the town is on a bend of the Marne, they mistook it for Villeneuve-Saint-Georges, which is on a bend of the Seine, and where there is a major rail network.

One of my new friends in Saint-Maur was the Parakeet. We couldn't figure out whether he was super smart or slightly touched in the head. My theory was that he was always ready to play the idiot to make others laugh, but that he was actually quite a bit smarter than most of the students. But sometimes, I swear, he really got into it, his role as an idiot. Most of the boys really liked him because he made them laugh. At school he could be the best and sometimes the worst of dunces. And even then it was hard to come to a consensus about what it was that made him go from top to bottom of the class.

One day the Parakeet and I were trying to solve a particularly thorny math problem (he really was the best at math); he stopped working all of a sudden, raised his eyes to the heavens and said, "Do you realize, Roger, this is "April 4th, April 4th, 1944". The fourth day of the fourth month, in the year 1944. We have to celebrate!"

We decided to leave our homework and do something really special. The only thing we could think of was to go and jump in the river, but the water was still icy. "We have to stay four minutes in the water, naturally!" shouted the Parakeet. Four minutes in the water on April 4th, it's not all that easy. But my companion felt that we had no choice if we wanted our gesture to have any significance at all. So we started counting, both of us, screaming louder and louder to give ourselves courage, up to 240. When we came out of the water we were all wound up. We rolled in the grass like animals to dry off, and then we put on our clothes as quick as we could, over our bodies covered in grass and sand. Then we jumped up and down to get warm, before collapsing exhausted on the ground.

"What a great idea that was! Can you imagine, Roger, we might not have thought of it, we might not have realized the date, or come up with such a good idea for a celebration."

"Yeah, that would've been a waste."

"A real waste, pal, a real wasteful waste wasted wastefully!"

We watched silently as the sun set.

"It would have been even better to go into the water just as the sun was disappearing below the horizon," said the Parakeet.

"Nothing is perfect. But you know what? We should do something special again together on May 5th, 1955."

"Yeah . . . but what? We may not even be in touch anymore . . . "

"Well, we can plan to meet all the same. We can decide on a place, a date . . . But we know that already, duh. And this time, we can make it at sunset."

I could tell that in his head the Parakeet was thinking as fast as I was, trying to find THE good idea.

"I know!" said my friend with a shout. "The Eiffel Tower!

On top of the Eiffel Tower, May 5th, 1955, at sunset. In eleven years, one month, and one day."

Nothing wrong with that. It was perfect. We looked at each other: our pact was sealed.

I didn't go to the meeting. On May 5th, 1955, I was in Moscow, a student at the University, and it wouldn't have been possible to ask for permission to go on such a "futile" trip to France. I never found out whether the Parakeet had gone up the Eiffel Tower or not. But if I had been in Paris that day, I would have shown up, beyond the shadow of a doubt.

June 7, 1944. First class that morning: French. Monsieur Noiret was already seated when we came in, which was not like him. He looked at us with a smile, then adopted a solemn expression.

"I can see, from your excitement, that you are already aware of the events that occurred during the night. I think it would be a good idea to devote some of the class to discussing them together."

We were all for it. As a rule, the adults preferred to tell us as little as possible, under the pretext that war wasn't good for children. But Monsieur Noiret knew that we weren't children anymore. And that we weren't quite adults, either.

"Right. The things that are happening at the moment are so important that they eclipse what you're learning at school—even literature, up to a point. For the time being, anyway . . . The Americans and their allies have finally decided to get seriously involved in the war. Something we've all been expecting for a long time. I think that this is a historical moment, that in a way this represents the beginning of the end for the Germans. I'm telling you this, something you already know, to emphasize the fact that there are soldiers from a number of different countries who, with their tanks and their weapons, landed in Normandy during the night. What is my point? It is that I was once your age, even though that might be difficult for you to imagine. And I know what idealism is, the desire to do something important, something heroic for one's country, that can fill the souls of young people like you. So to conclude . . . "

He broke off and looked around the classroom, pausing at length to stare at certain faces.

"To conclude, I want you to know that I believe we will be liberated soon. But also that anything you might do or not do will not change by one minute or one second the moment when that liberation comes. So I implore you, don't do anything stupid! Concentrate on your studies, and let the grown-ups get on with the war."

And he looked at us with his big gray eyes. I felt my cheeks burning . . . and my ears too. I lowered my head somewhat. Because he had not missed the mark, Monsieur Noiret, on the contrary. And I think I was not the only boy who knew he was on the money. I saw other lowered heads in front of me. It was true that I had given it some thought, and that we had spoken about it together, at night during the bombing, sitting up on the roof of our boarding house. That we had dreamed about it . . . I had even come up with a fairly precise plan. All I had to do was find a German officer and go up behind him without him noticing, grab his weapon, kill him, and then go off hunting for more German soldiers. It seemed normal to want to be a part of the liberation of France, to do my bit.

I wonder how many lives Monsieur Noiret saved that day.

CHAPTER 34

The Liberation Comes to Champagne

S ummer had arrived, vacation time, and I was delighted to go back to Paris where I hoped to be when the city was liberated. I had grasped Monsieur Noiret's point, and I had no intention of getting involved in anything, but I would have a front row seat for the show. Or at least, that's what I wanted.

No sooner did I reach my mother's place than she informed me that I would be going back to spend the summer with the Brisson family in Champagne. This was too much, she was going too far. It seemed to me that someday she would have to start taking my opinion into account regarding decisions that concerned me. But Lena was adamant.

"You are going, everything has been arranged."

"And if I refuse?"

"You won't refuse. This is not a suggestion, it's an order. You are going."

The argument went on late into the night. Two days later I was on the train to Épernay. Then another train as far as Mézy-Moulins. Where Albert was waiting for me with his horse and cart.

Back with the Brissons, I picked up my old habits from the previous summer. I saw Suzanne again, and she gave me some smiles that at least looked encouraging. But when I suggested going to the cinema, she gave me a funny look and told me she couldn't. Then she stood there before me, looking at me with her eyes wide open. So I ventured, "Well, maybe some other time?", less because I believed it than to fill the silence. She shrugged and walked away without answering. I had to resign myself that as far as this vacation was concerned, there would be no languorous kisses in the movie theater. Nor would it be Suzanne who helped me understand something about women.

Albert decided that I was big enough now to go with him to visit the villagers who wanted their pigs transformed into ham. Under the Occupation it was illegal to slaughter, sell, or eat one's own pigs, because they were meant for the German occupier. But who was about to go and inform on Albert or the people who hired him? As I had some experience in slaughtering rabbits, I was neither too impressed nor disgusted by all the blood. It was just the animal's cries as its throat was being cut that upset me. What I liked best of all were the delicious cutlets we brought home, which Yvonne made into a veritable feast.

Down at the bottom of the village some Germans were posted to keep watch over the locks. The war had been going on long enough for their French to be rather good. I made friends with a certain Dieter, and played dice with him (our local Germans made excellent partners for games, because in general they had nothing to do). He also taught me how to go fishing with hand grenades—there were a great many fish in the river, so when I got the feeling I hadn't done a bloody thing all day, I would ask Dieter to go fishing with me and I took a few fish home to the Brissons. Dieter also became my swimming instructor.

I was in the middle of a meal, sitting in the Brissons' dining room, when I heard on the radio that there was an uprising in Paris. The police, sensing that the liberation was imminent, had begun firing on the Germans. People from the opposition, both communists and Gaullists, had joined in. Germans were being killed and arrested. Paris was seeing to its own liberation. We spent the day and part of the night listening to the news on the BBC.

Champagne was still occupied. But given the increasingly palpable tension that reigned, we could see that it was only a question of time. The German soldiers were leaving their cabins less and less frequently, which deprived me of my games of dice and fishing expeditions with Dieter.

One night I woke up with a start. There was shouting, banging, the sound of footsteps. I could hear cries of "*Schnell, schnell,*" and other orders I couldn't understand. I rushed over to the window to look out. German soldiers seemed to be arriving from every side all at the same time, requisitioning everything in their path that might be useful: horses, bicycles, even donkeys. They went on shouting, pouring through the village all night long, then they disappeared shortly before dawn.

In the morning it was dead silent in Mont-Saint-Père. It was as if a hurricane had blown through there. The soldiers hadn't hurt anyone, all they'd wanted was to find vehicles or animals so they could get out of there. Albert looked around glumly then turned to Yvonne and said, "I'll bet that's the last time any German soldiers go through here." And he was right.

A few days later we could hear the American tanks just on the other side of the Marne. I wondered if they were going to forget us, because even though they were right nearby there was no indication they would be coming our way.

At around noon, the forest at the top of the hill seemed to come alive. We saw people coming out of the woods from all sides, again and again. Among them there were some people I recognized, whom I had seen the previous summer but hadn't seen again since coming back to Champagne. So they'd been hiding in the woods, with the partisans! The group headed toward the locks, toward the Germans' hut. They were all armed with rifles. It was war, of course, but still, I wished they could have spared those Germans we used to talk to, the ones I went fishing with, and who had never hurt anyone around here. I got the impression that behind me the entire village was waiting, transfixed.

Suddenly the Germans came out of their hut, with their hands in the air, shouting, "*Hitler, kaput!*" And all hell broke loose. Some of the partisans slowed their pace when they heard this anti-Hitler cry, others, on the contrary, got all excited, as if it were an affront. They kept walking, even more determined. The leader of the group went up to one of the Germans. He began by kicking him, a first time, and then again. The German didn't budge. A woman behind me called out, "Don't kill them!" And another added, "Don't hurt them!" The young partisan hesitated. Other voices were raised, all begging for mercy. The boy gave a last kick, harder than the previous ones, then he walked away, disgusted. Then the partisans made the Germans go up into the village. When they reached the main street, I went up to Dieter. It made me feel bad to see him there, so close to me, humiliated, with his hands on his head. He gave me a big smile. To which I replied with a timid one.

"You know why we still here?"

"Uh . . . no."

"Because we not stupid. We are intelligent." And he laughed a bit before he went on, "One day we must receive call by the telephone. One day, is sure. Telephone to say go to front, go find German army and continue war. And our sergeant, is sure, when order comes, he obey. So in secret we cut telephone wire . . . and Sergeant waits call. And waits. And waits. But never the telephone rings."

And there he gave a hearty laugh. Like a pupil who has played a nasty trick on his teacher.

I was still standing next to Dieter, laughing with him, when I heard a rumbling sound in the distance. Getting louder. With the other boys, I ran to the top of the hill. And we could see a dozen American tanks heading toward the village. We came back down, screaming, "The Americans are coming! The Americans are here!" We were euphoric. All the anxiety and tension we had felt for days now, even weeks, exploded in shouts of joy and chanting, we were jumping up and down, hugging, dancing. And I understood that this was it, that we at last we had been liberated! A first American tank appeared in the distance at the entrance to the village. The partisans shoved the Germans from the lock in the direction of the tank, which must have been going five kilometers an hour not to crush the crowds of people in the street. The American officer to whom the Germans were handed over did not even take the time to look at them. He couldn't care less about this handful of Jerries, who didn't look particularly dangerous.

Now the entire village was out in the street, surrounding the American tanks. They couldn't move any farther forward. Albert the Pig took me to one side and gave me the keys to the cellar.

"Go and fetch as many bottles of champagne as you can carry."

It took me a few seconds to understand what he was asking. Ever since I had come back to stay with the Brisson family, there had been a shortage of champagne. And yet, from time to time, Yvonne would ask Albert if he was sure there wasn't a bottle or two somewhere. I couldn't understand why she kept asking him, and found that she was curiously insistent. It was because she knew her husband well, and she must have suspected him of having put some in reserve for the end of the war.

"Go on, what are you waiting for, do I have to wind you up to get you to move a little?"

"Uh, no, I'm on my way, right now."

I filled baskets with bottles that I took back to Albert a few at a time. And he handed them out left and right so that everyone would have the pleasure of tossing them to the liberators. The Americans tossed plenty of things at us as well: chocolate, cigarettes, and soap (real soap, that lathered!). One of the most unpleasant things about the war had been the soap. There was nothing but that gray, clayey stuff which did not lather at all. So real soap, that smelled of perfume to boot, was to me an unmistakable sign: the war really was over now.

I could see Albert pointing at me with his finger. Someone ran up to me.

"You speak English, don't you?"

"Uh, I learned some at the lycée, yes."

"Well, one of them, the colonel, is saying stuff in English and we don't understand, and he seems to want us to find him an interpreter."

"I don't speak very much . . . "

"I doubt there is anyone here who speaks better. And anyway, you just have to understand what he's saying, you won't have to talk to him."

So they led me up to the colonel.

"Hello, my boy. So you're the one who speaks English, right?"

Oh no! I knew Americans had an accent, but not as strong as that! I didn't understand a thing except for "hello" and "English." But it was enough for me to reply with a timid little "yes."

"Okay, so can you explain to these people that I would like to eat some eggs?"

I must have looked completely lost, because then he said, articulating exaggeratedly, "To eat. FRESH EGGS!"

That word I knew, eggs, there could be no doubt about it. I turned to Albert and explained that the Americans wanted to eat some eggs. Albert waved his hands and told me to tell him they could come to his house.

"You come. This is Albert. Come with Albert for eggs."

One thing was for sure: I would never be an interpreter.

So there we were with a dozen American soldiers at our table. Yvonne made omelets for them while Albert poured champagne for everyone. As the evening progressed they had less need of my services, because the more they drank, the better the Americans and the French understood each other.

And that is how the American advance got as far as our village. During the evening, someone tried to explain to the Americans that there were some German tanks just near there, roughly four kilometers away, and I was translating, saying, "four kilometers" and pointing the same direction as our informant. And they told me to add, "They wait for you."

"Well, they can wait," replied the colonel. He went outside with his radio and talked for a few minutes. Then he came back in and asked for some more champagne.

Roughly an hour later, planes flew over the village. Then there was the sound of machine gun fire, along with explosions. It came from the direction I had indicated to the American colonel. It would seem that the German tanks weren't waiting after all.

Two days later, when the Americans had finally resolved to leave our ever so hospitable village, a black Citroën Traction pulled up outside the Brisson house. On the car there were big letters that said "FTP," which stood for "Francs-tireurs et Partisans." And I suddenly realized they had come for me.

I ran to pack my suitcase and went quickly around the village to say goodbye to everyone. Yvonne gave me a big hug and despite all her efforts she could not hold back her tears. Albert took me in his arms and said, "Roger, you worked very hard for us. You deserve a reward."

He went back into the house, walking slowly and heavily, in spite of the rising impatience of the people who had come to get me. He came back with a big sack of potatoes, as a souvenir, and Lena would surely be happy with it. I gave my last hugs and kisses to Yvonne and Albert and climbed into the big black car. I was quite sad to be leaving, but I was eager to get back to free Paris.

D on't you realize! I missed everything, everything! I missed the battle for Paris. I knew I should stay here, that I shouldn't let you send me to Champagne!"

I had only just arrived at Lena's lodgings.

"Hello, my son."

"I'm sorry . . . hello, Lena."

"Well. Yes, it's true, you missed it, but everything went fine without you."

"I'm not an idiot! I just wanted to be here, to see all the excitement, I don't know . . . it was a historical moment, after all! And I missed it because of you!"

"You've lived through a lot of historical moments, ever since you were born. And here, it was too dangerous. That was why I sent you to Champagne."

"What?"

"I knew there will be battle. And I knew that you, like all boys your age, you will want to get involved. And you know, it worked, but it was lucky. And there was many casualties, hundreds of dead. It wasn't worth risking your life foolishly, almost the end of the war."

Her words reminded me of what Monsieur Noiret had said in class. Except that my mother had belonged to the Resistance, and she had risked her life. And surely, by virtue of that alone, she must have risked my life at times, too. But it was too late now, it was done, Paris was free.

Lena handed me a navy blue suit: "It's for you, put it on." I looked at it: the jacket was from the FTP! I felt like a bit of an imposter, but my pride in wearing it won out. And when I walked around the streets in Paris, people would greet me and give me a kindly smile. I was a war hero.

Life was no longer dangerous in Paris. Food was still rationed, but we didn't have to hide, there was no longer any risk we might be arrested. Since I had to go back to Saint-Maur-des-Fossés for my studies, I kept my identity as Roger Binet. I didn't know how much longer I would be able to live like that, for when I went to apply for my ID card, someone somewhere might eventually realize that there were two Roger Binets born on August 3, 1929, in Versailles. On the other hand, if I resumed my identity as Julian Kryda, I'd have no papers proving that I had successfully completed my first years at the lycée, and I'd have no legal status in France. Every time I talked it over with Lena, we came to a dead end, and she kept saying she would think about it later.

I managed to convince her not to send me back to the fat bearded man, Monsieur Barbier. She found me a place in the country with the Dłuski family: Ostap, Stasia and their son Wiktor. These were people Lena had known in the Communist Party back in Poland. At the beginning of the Occupation, after she had warned them that there was going to be a raid in their neighborhood, they had lived with us for a while on the rue Aubriot.

Roughly one week after I arrived at their big house, Wiktor, who was now six years old, came up and stared at me for a long time.

"You know, I know a boy who looks a lot like you. Really a lot. But he doesn't have the same name as you."

"Really? What's his name?"

"Jules. I used to live with him, and he played with me the way you do. I don't suppose you know him by any chance?"

"Well, can you imagine, I do know him. He's my brother. It's true we look a lot alike."

"And where is he, now?"

"He goes to school in another town, so he can't live with you."

"I'd like him to come and visit someday. I want to play with him again."

"I'll tell him, I promise."

Yes, I know, not a great idea to say he was my brother. And I don't think I convinced my little Wiktor. But I couldn't tell him the truth, he was too young, it was too risky, he might not know how to keep the secret, and everyone knew me as Roger Binet, now. Out of all the lies I'd had to tell during the war, this lie to Wiktor was hardest of all. Probably because I sensed that he didn't believe me and he was disappointed to see I was lying to him, because he wanted me to be a friend he could trust.

On my days off, I went back to Lena's place, as I had a lot to do in Paris. I was now a bona fide member of the movement of young communists of France, the MJCF. Every Sunday I distributed our newspaper. I would walk through the streets and the parks, or go into buildings, and shout, "Get it here, read *L'Avant-Garde*, the newspaper of the young communists of France! Get it here, read *L'Avant-Garde*, the newspaper of the young communists of France!" I found I had a talent for selling and very quickly I was put in charge of selling the paper in the third arrondissement.

One Sunday, during a communist youth demonstration, I was walking proudly with my sign, "France to the People," when suddenly we heard a deafening, terrifying, whistling sound in the sky. Everyone stopped, stunned, looking skyward. Someone shouted, "It's V2 missiles, run for cover!" (The V2 was a German missile that could reach Paris from as far away as the Netherlands. It was a new weapon that the Germans were only just beginning to use, and Hitler was sure that it would enable him to win the war.) The crowd went into a panic, everyone was running every which way looking for shelter. We were used to rockets and air raids. But with this thundering noise you really got the impression that this time all of Paris was about to explode.

It was dark in my shelter. There were seven or eight of us who had run this far, and right next to me was a young girl who was about my age. I could just make out her terrified eyes. I smiled at her. She tried to return my smile, but her lips were trembling. Suddenly, we could no longer hear the whistling noise. The girl looked at me, even more terrified. I moved closer to her and put my arms around her. And then there was an explosion, in the distance. And the sound of sirens from the emergency vehicles getting louder and louder. Obeying an impulse that came out of nowhere, I put my lips on the girl's. She didn't resist. On the contrary, she relaxed into my arms.

People in the street were rushing this way and that. My neighbor from the shelter and I looked at each other and tacitly agreed to let other people worry about the urgency of the situation, and we would go on getting acquainted. We stayed for roughly an hour in the shelter of the porte cochère, and when the calm had returned all around us, we parted, not even bothering to tell each other our names.

E arly May, 1945. It was a holiday. It was my intention to take part in the big May Day demonstration, but for the time being, I was lounging on my little camp bed in the single room that made up Lena's lodgings.

I could hear footsteps in the corridor. Trudging, and slightly out of sync. I leapt out of bed when I heard someone knock on the door. Lena opened it, froze, put her hand to her mouth, took it away, remained motionless for a few moments then eventually cried out: "Arnold!"

"Arnold? You're mistaken. I'm Roger Colombier. So, how is my wife Hélène doing these days?"

It really was him. We hadn't seen him in . . . could it have been three years? We hadn't even known whether he was still alive. And there he was, making jokes. He and Lena began speaking Polish. And Arnold looked at me. Silence. I could tell he was moved. He held out his arms. I hurried over as quickly as my adolescent body would allow.

"My little Roger!"

"My big Roger!"

I tried to joke the way he did, but it wasn't easy. Tall, imposing Arnold had little more than skin on his bones. He was wearing the striped clothing of a prisoner from a concentration camp. That was what we'd been afraid of, that he been taken to a camp. The good news was that he was alive, but I didn't expect to see him looking so emaciated.

"Come on, come on, my little Roger, get dressed right away. We're going to the demonstration."

While I was getting ready, Lena offered him some tea and cookies. When I was ready I sat down at the table, took a few cookies and observed Arnold. Obviously he had lost weight, but the hardest thing to see was his eyes. His big blue eyes that had always had a mischievous twinkle in them were now . . . I don't know . . . it was as if a light had gone out. They were faded. Sad. No, defeated.

"Well, are you ready? You took your time! Are you coming with us, Lena?"

"No, I have to wait for Annette, I promised her we'd go together. But don't wait for me, *nie czekajcie na mnie.*"

I walked at the head of the procession, next to Arnold, with other survivors from the camps, all wearing their striped clothing. All of France seemed to be parading through the streets of Paris, from the place de la Bastille to the place de la Nation. I was proud to be there, among those who had known which was the right side to be on and, risking their lives, had chosen that side. You could feel the great emotion, the exaltation, in the crowd. It was as if my heart were about to explode—I wished I could have started running so that the movement of my body would correspond to the beating of my heart. But I didn't want to leave Arnold behind.

A few weeks later, it was Geneviève's turn to come back. She too had lost a lot of weight, and she had the same look in her eyes as Arnold. They told us what had happened to them. Briefly.

Arnold was imprisoned at Buchenwald. Now at last I learned why Lena had lost touch with him: he had left the Resistance to start dealing in the black market. That was why he got arrested. The Germans never even knew that he was Jewish and communist. Once he was at the camp, his knowledge of French, Polish, German, and Russian singled him out to play an important role. And thanks to his training as a radio engineer, he managed to build a little receiving set with crystals so he could listen to the BBC. Then he presented the news from the front in a clandestine bulletin which he distributed among the other prisoners. After he returned to France, certain members of the Communist Party didn't want to let him back into their ranks because of his desertion from the Resistance. But others convinced them to take him back—they figured he had redeemed himself with his clandestine work at the camp.

Geneviève had been detained in two prisons in France, then the Germans sent her to Ravensbrück, a camp for women. The conditions there were very harsh. She found herself among criminals, prostitutes, Catholics, and Jews. And very few communists. Even though she had no one to talk politics with, Geneviève had been fascinated by this micro society made up of so many different women. That was all she would agree to talk about.

May 8, 1945. Germany had signed the instrument of surrender. For a few weeks there were celebrations and demonstrations practically nonstop. The country was jubilant. Very moved by Arnold and Geneviève's stories, I offered my services to the communist youth to go to the train stations in order to meet the prisoners coming back from the camps. We had to give them métro tickets, a square meal, and some money, and we helped the weakest ones to get where they had to go. Sometimes we would take them to our MJCF offices, for as long as it took for them to find their family, or friends they could go to.

Most of the people returning from the camps had already had medical treatment, and they'd been fed and regained some strength before returning to France. The ones I greeted didn't look like those living skeletons I saw not long afterwards, once the photos the journalists had taken upon the liberation of the camps started to appear.

Geneviève and Arnold found a little apartment. That summer of 1945, they managed to get in touch with a few former pupils from L'Avenir Social, and on the first day of vacation they invited us to come to a party at their house. There were six of us in all, including . . . Rolande. With her sister Élise. And Philippe. And a certain Christian, who was older than me, and he was in uniform because he was leaving for Indochina the very next day. And there was Daniel, whom I used to think of as a "little kid" at the time, and who was twelve years old now.

Rolande was still just as beautiful, with a new self-confidence and a slightly irreverent sense of humor that I liked a lot. After the colony, she had gone to live with her aunt in Vendée. She wasn't happy there. Shortly before the liberation of Paris, she managed to get a letter to Simone, one of our old instructors from L'Avenir Social, and Simone had agreed to take her in. So she'd had the extreme good fortune to experience first-hand what I was so miserable at having missed.

My faint memories of Christian were of a solitary and silent boy. Now he talked too much. He didn't have a lot to say about his life during the war, but preferred to talk about Indochina. He thought the French administration of the colony must be defended at any cost. This led to a long discussion, which Geneviève brought to an end just before it degenerated, bringing out a delicious carrot cake.

Philippe's manner had acquired a layer of cynicism which, in the long run, was irritating. He told us how he had convinced his parents to let him to join the Resistance. He had worked as a messenger toward the end of the war, when news had to be carried very quickly, and he wrote articles for the newspaper *Défense de la France.* He was determined to go into politics after his studies.

I decided not to say anything about the fact that I had spent part of the war living under an assumed name, one that everyone there was familiar with. So for the space of an evening I was Jules once again—Julot for Geneviève. It felt strange when Rolande asked if anyone had had any news from Roger and Pierre Binet. But no one had any news.

All those stories kept us up late, so we stayed overnight at Geneviève and Arnold's place.

A few days later, Lena came into the apartment with an expression on her face I'd never seen. There were tears in her eyes and she could hardly breathe.

"What's going on?"

"Oh, my Julek, *mój kochany!* Do you know who I heard from?"

"Well, no."

She sat down, and began to cry. Then to laugh. I was beginning to worry about her mental state when finally she said, "I've had a letter from your father. Through Anna. We've had news from Emil."

Every time I had asked her about Emil, Lena said more or less the same thing: he was a soldier in the Russian army, fighting at the front. Now, in the uninterrupted stream of words coming out of her mouth, I understood that in fact, she hadn't had any news for several years, and she didn't know whether he was alive, or whether he'd started another life elsewhere, or whether he even thought about us sometimes. So now, to find out that he was alive, and back in Poland, and that he'd been moving heaven and earth to get in touch with us, was beyond anything she had ever dared hope for.

"He is back in Warsaw, and he went to Fruzia's, who has address of their sister Anna. So, she sent letter."

"And what does he say in his letter?"

"Wait, I make quick translation: 'My dear Lena and Julek, you must wonder if I am still alive. Yes, I am. Just barely, I am back in Poland, and they tell me you are in France. I want to see you again. I have much to tell you, too much to write here. Write to me and tell me if you are going to come back to Poland, now that war is over. I send you big hugs and kisses from Emil, your ghost."

Lena and I sat there for a few minutes without saying a thing. Thoughts were whirling in my head. I had never seen Emil since learning he was my father. But I had always liked him, you might even say that I felt close to him. At the same time, what could remain of a closeness I had felt when I was four or five years old, now that I was fifteen? I had often wondered whether I would ever see him again, and I'd hoped I would, but I had been growing increasingly doubtful. I could not say that I'd missed him, it made me sadder to think about Fruzia and Hugo. But one thing was for sure, I had never imagined going back to Poland to live, a country where I couldn't even speak the language anymore. I was a proper Frenchman now, and even somewhat nationalistic about it.

"We'll have to think about it. Not right away, but soon. Whether we want to go back to Poland."

"You can do what you want, but I'm staying here. I'm French. Next year I have the first baccalaureate exam, I can't go to school in Poland, it's out of the question."

"I understand. But we'll think about it and talk about it later. Okay?"

Two days later, Lena had a proposal for me. One I could not refuse. We would go and spend the summer vacation in Poland. And after that, we would come back to Paris, unless we both agreed to stay in Poland. And she served up a sledge-hammer argument: we would make the trip in a Soviet war-plane.

To take a plane! The trip was worth it for that alone. And basically I was happy to know I would see Emil, Fruzia, and

Hugo again. We would be leaving a few days after the national holiday on July 14.

This was the first postwar Bastille Day. The parade in Paris was grandiose, practically gigantic. I was very proud, personally, because I had the good fortune of parading next to an American soldier. I don't know how, but he had showed up a few days earlier at Tobcia and Beniek's place. Since his last name was Rappoport, I think that he must have been some vague cousin of Lena and her sisters. He spoke Yiddish with Tobcia and my mother. But with me he spoke English. That's how I ended up, on the French national holiday, speaking English with an American cousin.

Four days later, on July 18, Annette came to drive Lena and me to the airport at Le Bourget, where we would board our flight to Poland, sitting on the floor in a Soviet warplane that had no seats, a Tupolev. There were other people too, a dozen passengers in all. The plane took off, lifting heavily from the ground, up it went, then came down a little bit, then up again. The engines made a deafening sound, preventing any conversation until the plane reached its cruising speed high in the sky. We were shaken, tossed, knocked back and forth. I looked at Lena, and I am sure that throughout the entire war, all those years of clandestinity, she had never been so terrified. The expression *as white as a sheet* fit her perfectly just then; I wish I could come up with something more original, but sometimes you just have to go with what is patently obvious.

Once we were settled in up above the clouds, we were able to speak with our fellow passengers. I talked mainly with a Polish lady, Sophie, who had been with the International Brigades in Spain. She told me about her war, which was very different from mine.

We flew above Germany. Then we were in Poland. The plane began to lose altitude. Lena went her alabaster color again. Everyone tried to find a spot at the window to watch as we landed in Warsaw. The weather was magnificent, and the view was perfect. When we saw the city, everyone stopped breathing. It was terrible. Unreal. There was nothing left. Nothing. Ruins, just ruins, everywhere. No one could think of a single word, there was no way to describe what all of us were seeing at the same time. Some began to weep in silence.

We landed at Warsaw airport. From there we were taken to the Hotel Polonia, the first obligatory stop for people who didn't know where to go in the devastated city. Since we knew that Emil had managed to find Fruzia and Hugo, we would be going to their house. There were lots of horses and carts outside the hotel, with coachmen calling out their destinations: *Na Boliborz, na Boliborz! Na Prage, na Prage!* We took one that was headed for *Joliboge* (or so it sounded to my French ears).

The most direct route was straight through the Warsaw ghetto. What was left of it. I had thought there would be no greater shock than the one we'd had as the plane was landing over Warsaw. But I was wrong. Warsaw was devastated, yet there were a few buildings standing here and there, there were still streets that defined limits. But in the ghetto there was nothing. Not even streets. Everything was crushed, flattened. The horse picked its way through the rubble along the path that had been cleared by repeated passage. A powerful odor of corpses filled our nostrils. A halo of dust floated over the ruins.

The building where I had spent my Polish childhood had not been destroyed. Boliborz, oddly enough, seemed to have been spared. I felt all wobbly inside. I knew every step in the stairway. I knew there were twenty between each landing. I resisted the desire to count them. The walls had aged, of course, but some of the marks I remembered were still there, just the same but darker. The stairs were full of rubble. We climbed up to the top floor and knocked on the door of number 23.

Hugo opened the door. And froze, his hand before his lips,

like Lena a few days earlier when she saw tall, emaciated Arnold. Was this the most common, most oft-repeated gesture, after the end of the war? He called out to Fruzia. She cried out, seemed to hesitate between throwing arms around Lena, hugging me (but I was so tall now that she didn't know where to put her arms), and collapsing into tears. She chose to combine the first and last options, and burst into tears in Lena's arms. Hugo spoke to me. Lena hurried to explain the inexplicable: I no longer spoke Polish. Or at least that was what I took her words to mean when I saw Hugo and Fruzia's stunned expression.

There was one question I was dying to ask: did Hugo receive a lighter I sent to him way back at the beginning of my stay in France, as part of my strategy to inform him I'd been kidnapped? Lena had forgotten the episode and conveyed my request to Hugo quite candidly. He shook his head. For that I needed no translation. How many times had Lena betrayed me in this way?

On the wall in the kitchen someone had written in tall black letters: *Kapitan Michał Gruda*, with the number of his military posting. It was my father: he had come to Hugo and Fruzia's place, found no one in the apartment, and left this message. Lena burst out laughing.

"I've often wondered what our names would be. Well, I think the matter is settled! Since your father's name is still Gruda, you will be Julian Gruda, as you were when you were born."

Even though I was happy to see Hugo and Fruzia again, I was restless in their presence, because conversation was difficult, and I didn't like having to turn to my mother all the time. Besides, I suspected she did not translate my words very accurately, or those of my former parents. I was eager to explore Warsaw, or what was left of it. But I could understand that after all these years apart we couldn't just have a cup of tea for twenty minutes and then leave. So I listened, and tried to see what I could make out from these long processions of words, whether there were any that were familiar. Hugo seemed to notice my restlessness. During a spell of silence, he looked at me, winked, stood up and left the room. I turned and looked at Fruzia, who shrugged, as if to tell me she had no idea what he had gone to do. Hugo came back holding something that looked like a photograph. He handed it to me. Dear Lord! I had never found out whether he had paid the photographer, and I was sure that the photo had never been developed, and we'd never received it. But there they all were, all the friends from my first life. And I was right in the middle, looking very serious, a simple little Polish boy who was living with the people he thought were his parents. I remembered the names of all the children my age. I sat there for a long time looking at the photograph, very moved.

It was decided that Lena and I would stay there until another option became available. I wanted to walk around the town on my own, and so Lena wrote a note on a piece of paper: *Mieszkam na ßoliborzu, WSM, Kolonia 5. Przepraszam, ale nie rozumiem po polsku.* Which said, "I live in ßoliborz, WSM (for Warsaw Habitation Cooperative), Colony 5. I am sorry but I don't speak Polish." After a few days, I didn't need the paper anymore, I knew how to say those two sentences.

And at the beginning of August, at Hugo and Fruzia's place, Emil showed up. He and Lena embraced somewhat awkwardly. They looked at each other for a long time, not saying anything. Where to begin, after so long? Silence seemed a good solution to me. They hugged a second time, a bit less awkwardly, a bit more tenderly. Then Emil turned to me. He smiled. Pursed his lips and closed his eyes, as if to hold back his tears. He came over to me and began to speak.

"*Przepraszam, ale nie rozumiem po polsku,*" was what I said, with my heavy French accent, but I was rather proud that I had learned a bit of Polish so quickly.

You would have thought I had just informed him that his entire family had died! I've never seen anyone's mood change so abruptly. His eyes opened wide and filled with horror. He turned to Lena, and began to yell at her, really yell!

"What? He doesn't speak Polish anymore? What were you thinking? Honestly, I prepared myself for every eventuality—that my son might be crippled. Handicapped. Disfigured. An idiot, even. But never, never could I have imagined that he would no longer understand Polish. What were you thinking? How could you have let such a thing happen?"

And wasn't that a lovely reunion for a couple who hadn't seen each other in ten years?

The next day, Lena informed me that Emil was coming to pick me up and that we'd be taking the train. He wanted me to go with him to visit the place where he worked. He hoped to get to know me that way, and create a bond between father and son. I had no objections. It was on a train that Lena had informed me that I was her son. So it seemed fitting that it was on a train that Emil was going to try to become my father.

When Emil came to the door, he reached into a big bag and took out a Polish army uniform and asked me to put it on. He was wearing his captain's uniform (from the Polish army, too, because he never was in the Red Army, as my mother had said). Apparently it would be easier for me to get around in an army uniform. So it was as a soldier that I had my first outing with my real father.

CHAPTER 38
The Trip with Emil

We climbed aboard a train packed with Polish and Russian soldiers. My father knew a few of them, and he introduced me to them with a mixture of pride and embarrassment—because of my linguistic handicap. The journey seemed endless; I got completely fed up with nodding my head whenever anyone spoke to me, and pretending to understand what they were saying. And the train moved at a snail's pace: we stopped in fields, we stopped in stations. Soldiers climbed on, others got off. Later, my father would explain that the trip from Warsaw to Poznan, which normally took three hours, had lasted almost twenty.

My feelings toward Emil were ambivalent. I didn't know him at all, and felt no attachment to him, but there was nevertheless this little something inside me, a feeling of recognition. I was eager to know who this man was, what he thought, how he expressed himself. I noticed that he often made the other soldiers laugh, even without acting the clown. I could sense a sharp intelligence and great sensitivity. In short, I had a lot of time to spy on the man I knew was my father.

At last we arrived in Poznan. A woman officer was waiting for us at the station. She was with her daughter, Basia, a pretty girl roughly my age, her round face adorned with dimples and almond-shaped eyes. We settled into their little two-room apartment. For how long? I had no idea. The girl and I couldn't say anything to each other, at least with words. So we found another language, a more tactile one. So far, I liked traveling with my father.

We stayed in Poznan for a few days. Initially I had been under the impression that Emil was here on a military mission. But as we spent most of our time at the lady's apartment, I eventually understood that his mission was more personal than professional.

One morning Emil came to get me. Our stay in Poznan was over. I put on my soldier's uniform, packed my bag and gave Basia one last kiss. And we left for the station, where we took the train for Wrocław. We got there in the middle of the night, after a long journey. There were several groups of soldiers at the station, as many Russians as there were Poles. My father went over to a group of Poles. After that he motioned me over, and we sat down on the cement ground. My father explained something to me, still in Polish, because he hadn't accepted the fact that I couldn't understand a thing. I gathered we'd be spending the night there. I made a pillow with my bag and after a good hour I managed to fall asleep. I don't know how long I had been asleep when another train came into the station. Some soldiers got off. Emil talked with them for a quarter of an hour or so. Then he came and sat back down next to me. I fell asleep again. Another train came in, with more soldiers. And the same scenario all over: my father got up, they all huddled together and talked . . . This time, my father came back and motioned to me to get up.

All the soldiers took their guns out of their holsters and we left the station together. It was pitch dark in the town, except for occasional flashes of light, accompanied by the sound of explosions. We could hear isolated gunshots. I got the impression that the news the war was over had not traveled this far. We made our way slowly into Wrocław. Another group of soldiers suddenly came around the corner in the dark. We stopped short. All the soldiers raised their guns. Long minutes went by. In all those years of conflict, this was the closest I had ever come to anything remotely resembling real warfare. And it was happening now that the war was over. Or at least, I had thought it was over.

After a while, one man left our group. He was holding a flashlight and he shone it on his face. From the other side, a soldier started walking toward us, also shining his flashlight on his face. They stood directly facing each other. All eyes were glued on them. They exchanged some papers. Finally they shook hands and embraced one another. There was laughter from both camps, and everyone put their guns away.

Our envoy came back to inform us that it was a detachment of Russian soldiers, not German, as we had feared. We went over to them, everyone shook hands and patted each other on the shoulders. Our group set off for the city hospital. And that's where Emil and I ended up staying.

My father was very busy at the hospital, even though I didn't understand the exact nature of his activities there. He visited the patients, wounded soldiers for the most part, and spoke with them, filled out papers for them, and had discussions with the hospital management.

Since the beginning of our train journey, I hadn't been feeling very well. I was aching all over, and I felt weak. And now I was in a bad way. All my joints were painful and I was finding it more and more difficult to walk. Emil didn't seem to be taking my state very seriously, and tried to cure me with shots of pepper vodka. But eventually he had to face facts: whether he believed my illness was serious or not, I had reached a point where I could hardly walk straight. He wasn't worried exactly, but he saw he could no longer force me to go along with him: he would have to do something and have a doctor look at me. He dragged me out to a car and only managed to get me inside it with great effort. There was no position where I felt comfortable, and I seemed to hurt all over, all the time.

I don't know why Emil didn't simply have a doctor from

the hospital in Wrocław examine me instead of taking me by car, when I was in pain, hours away from the town of Łód , where I was taken directly to the military hospital.

The doctor who examined me had studied in Paris and spoke fluent French—that did me a world of good! He loved it when I used slang, even though he didn't understand everything; he actually spoke astonishingly colloquial French himself for someone who rolled his r's the way he did. And while he was learning new words of Parisian slang I was quietly learning Polish again with the help of some kind nurses, who saw to it that I spent several hours a day in a heating device. But my aches did not go away.

One of the first words of Polish I learned at the hospital was *pluskwa*. I was with a dozen other patients in the same ward. My first night at the hospital, when it was time for bed, the patient in the next bed tried to explain something to me, waving his arms. I understood *noc* (night) and a few other words, but not the whole message. One word came back on a regular basis, this word *pluskwa*, but I had no idea what it was referring to.

When everybody was in bed, they switched off the lights. I tried to find a comfortable position in my bed, in spite of the pain. A few seconds later, the lights came back on, and all the patients sat up abruptly and began pounding on their beds with their bedroom slippers. They gestured to me to do likewise. I set about it somewhat halfheartedly, and then I saw little red dots spring up all over my sheets. Now I got it: *pluskwa* meant "bedbug." Every night we had to go through the same rigmarole, as clearly it was not the final solution for getting rid of the critters.

After a few days had gone by, my doctor came to me with the diagnosis: rheumatic fever.

"Bloody fucking hell! Where did you pick that up?"

He examined the back of my throat closely.

"Your tonsils look healthy. So we'll remove them."

"What?"

"I bet that will get rid of the pain! It's often a bacteria due to tonsillitis that attacks the joints. So we'll do it right away, although the nurse is on leave . . . "

And that is how I found myself assisting on my own operation. The doctor explained that he absolutely needed my help, because there was a shortage of nurses in the hospital. He made me learn the names of all the instruments, explaining that I would have to hand them to him as he asked for them one after the other.

"If you get the wrong instrument, it could be serious, I might botch the operation. You have to concentrate. I'll only give you a local anesthesia, so you'll have all your wits about you. Do you think you are up to it?"

"Of course."

"You're not going to be scared stiff?"

My pride prevented me from showing just how terrified I was. At the time I did not realize that his method aimed to make me forget fear and pain, because there was indeed a shortage of nurses, and he had nothing in the way of effective anesthesia. It hardly mattered, I took my job very seriously and had my tonsils removed, by what was virtually cold surgery, and I was neither bound nor in pain, so focused was I on my work as an assistant, since any error on my part could have disastrous consequences.

"You see your tonsils? They look like they're in perfect condition. Hang on a moment, I'm just going to cut them . . . "

I watched attentively. The interior of my tonsils was full of pus. It was disgusting to think I'd had that in my throat for god knows how long.

"You see? I was right. You're going to start to feel better, but you've had a nasty illness, and while it might have only licked at your joints, it has bitten your heart."

"What do you mean?"

"You'll have to go easy on your heart. You have to forget about sports, and settle for a job that doesn't require physical effort—something in an office, sitting on your butt."

"But why?"

"Your heart has been affected, there's no doubt; that's the way it is, it will always be weak."

The thing was, I really had no desire to spend my life sitting on my butt. I wanted to become a great journalist and travel all over the world and file reports.

As the doctor had predicted, the pain in my joints soon disappeared. And I was just as fit as before. I decided not to pay any attention to his advice; I wouldn't allow that idiotic illness that had only lasted a few weeks to dictate my future.

Back in Warsaw, it was time for major decisions. My mother had promised we would go back to Paris, but I could tell she had no intention of doing so. Lena felt at home, now that Poland was communist, and she had no desire to go back to a country that wasn't. At first I was furious, because if I had followed her all the way to Poland, it was precisely because she had promised I could go back to France for my studies. At the same time, it was normal for her to want to live with my father. Since he worked for the Polish army and didn't know a word of French, it was out of the question for him to want to go and live in France.

So I decided to go back on my own. Given the fact I had no passport, either French or Polish, there were a few administrative things I had to take care of first. I wrote to Tobcia, because she was the only person I thought I could go and live with. And while I waited for her answer, I began the formalities to get my papers.

Tobcia was taking a long time to answer. Obtaining my papers was incredibly complicated. And Lena, meanwhile, was doing a very efficient and persuasive job with her propaganda.

"What will you live on? If I send you zlotys, you won't be

able to do a thing with them. And I just found a job in Łód . We could live there for a while, you could go to school in Polish. The destruction in Łód is not nearly as bad as in Warsaw, the atmosphere there would be quite different."

I have translated this conversation so that it would be in the same language as the rest of my story, but Lena spoke Polish to me now, because I could understand almost everything. Yet again, she managed to persuade me. I was not sure I wanted to stay in Poland forever, but I could see that for the time being going back to France was unrealistic. Once I was an adult, if I still wanted to, then I could go back. For my university studies, for example.

We were given a two room apartment in Łód , where my father, who had to travel from town to town for his work—he was a major now and in charge of an organization which helped demobbed soldiers reintegrate into civilian life—came to visit us from time to time. I was enrolled at the school, even though I had no papers—I was far from being the only one in such a situation. To enroll, all I had to do was give my name, date and place of birth. The administrators knew that my papers would come through someday, even though it might take a long time. I changed my life for the umpteenth time. A new life under the name of Julian Gruda. And that would remain my name for the rest of my days.

EPILOGUE

I'm on my way back to the house, just past the bridge, unmistakable with its green roof. My dog, Nez-Roux, is running ahead of me in circles. She still hasn't lost hope of winning a race against the cars. Spring has come early this year, too early, according to my neighbor, Mr. Harrison, who is worried about his thousands of daylilies. I can hear the cries of the huge flocks of white geese, returning from the warmth. There is no ice on the river by the house. That too is astonishing. Normally in the month of March there are chunks of ice of every size and shape rushing past.

I turned eighty-two this autumn. No doubt I am living the last of my many lives here in Sainte-Angèle-de-Laval, not far from Trois-Rivières, where I worked for thirty years at the university as a professor of biochemistry.

If someone had told me when I was little that when I grew up I would be a science professor! In the end, I studied animal physiology and biochemistry at the University of Moscow. Because even though I learned Polish again very quickly, I didn't master the written language sufficiently to study literature in Poland or become a journalist.

After I came back from Moscow I lived in Poland for many years, until 1968. I waited until my father died before I left the country. It would have been a hard blow for him; for all his life he remained a true patriot, and he would have seen my departure as a betrayal. Life can be astonishing. There I was, I had wanted to be a journalist in order to describe the virtues of communism, and among other things, I became a biochemist and fled from the Eastern Bloc. I lost my faith in 1956, when the Soviet tanks invaded Hungary.

Lena stayed in Poland until her death in 1989. She remained a member of the Communist Party until the rise of the Solidarity movement; she was carried away by the anti-communist fervor that reigned throughout the country, and in 1981 she handed in her party membership card.

I have to go and spend two weeks in France at the end of the month. There's no one left there from my childhood, from the days when I spoke the language of dogs. When you get old, there are bound to be fewer and fewer chances of finding the people you ran around with when you all wore short trousers. My daughters have made numerous attempts through the Internet to find Roger Binet. To no avail. They would have so liked to give me this present, even if it turned out that he was dead—at least to find out how he had lived, the boy whose identity enabled me to get through the war.

Last week was the eighth anniversary of Geneviève's death. She was a marvelous woman, all her life, involved socially and politically, always ready to help those less fortunate than her, and explain to her children and grandchildren everything they wanted to know about history, politics, literature . . . She never lost her patience, except in the face of injustice. Arnold did not age as well. Nevertheless I always considered him to be my spiritual, or rather my political father. He could be gruff, and sometimes downright disagreeable. But he was always pleased to see me, when from time to time I went to Poland for a visit, after I had moved to Quebec.

This is where the tale of my childhood ends, the chaotic childhood of a boy who knew how to speak the language of dogs. I'm looking forward to sharing it with my grandson, Émile—he's the one who is so very fond of raptors. He is the only one of my children and grandchildren who has inherited my gift for communicating with animals.

ABOUT THE AUTHOR

Born in Poland, Joanna Gruda arrived in Trois-Rivières, Canada, by boat at the age of two. She acted in the theater and worked as a comedian for many years, and she is a translator and an editor. *Revolution Baby* is her debut novel.